Justice o

James Watson is the author of novels and short
stories for young people, as well as educational
books and plays for radio. He combines writing
with lecturing in Media and Communication
studies. The winner of both the Other Award and
the Buxtehuder Bulle Prize, he is married and lives
in Tunbridge Wells, Kent.

Other books by James Watson

THE FREEDOM TREE
TALKING IN WHISPERS

Justice of the Dagger

James Watson

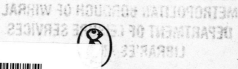

PUFFIN BOOKS

Published by the Penguin Group
Penguin Books Ltd, 27 Wrights Lane, London w8 5tz, England
Penguin Putnam Inc., 375 Hudson Street, New York, New York 10014, USA
Penguin Books Australia Ltd, Ringwood, Victoria, Australia
Penguin Books Canada Ltd, 10 Alcorn Avenue, Toronto, Ontario, Canada m4v 3b2
Penguin Books (NZ) Ltd, 182–190 Wairau Road, Auckland 10, New Zealand

Penguin Books Ltd, Registered Offices: Harmondsworth, Middlesex, England

First published 1998
1 3 5 7 9 10 8 6 4 2

Set in 11/13pt Monotype Palatino
Typeset by Rowland Phototypesetting Ltd,
Bury St Edmunds, Suffolk
Printed in England by Clays Ltd, St Ives plc

British Library Cataloguing in Publication Data
A CIP catalogue record for this book is available from the British Library

ISBN 0-141-30007-8

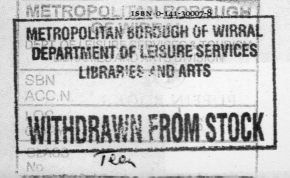

With warm thanks to
Chris Kloet,
my editor over many years

and in memory of
Muriel Barker (1905–97)

Contents

PROLOGUE

The high forest: night fever

Lyana knows this is a dream. She knows because in the dream the window of the compound will not open. How treacherous are dreams, for in real life she and Maria had prised the window open. Beyond was the high fence, the barbed wire and beyond that the open arms of the forest. They had run, as the dream will never permit her to run.

The ground was mud from the time of the typhoon; and then as if the escape plan had angered the gods because it was too perfect, too simple, too certain to succeed, the silence was broken by the shouts of the guards.

The dream always permitted this new scene: two girls throwing themselves to earth at the point below the fence where the storms had flushed out a narrow passage to liberty.

'Halt or we fire!' The voice of the officer threatens all the pain in the world.

Maria: 'We've got to stop.'

Lyana, who was the one to survive: 'Never!'

She awakes, shuddering, soaked in sweat. The eyes of Muyu, the chief's son, glint in the firelight. He stabs the fire with a stick. 'See,' he says, indicating the sparks that dance into the ice-cold air, 'that is what Mother Forest does with bad dreams!'

Lyana sighs. She loves Muyu but he is too young to understand. She shakes her head. 'Not this dream, Muyu.'

The capital: the burglar and the assassin

The last time Benni had been found breaking into Colonel Fario's office in the governor's residency he had been flogged so badly, his employers, the Island Security Force, had feared he would never spy for them again.

They had underestimated the healing power of the flesh, bones and spirit of Benni spelt with an 'i' as he always insisted on reminding people. He was back now, visiting old haunts – for Colonel Fario's cigars brought a high price in the markets of the capital.

Alas for Benni with an 'i', he has almost been caught once more. He had chatted his way past the guards at the main gate. He had slipped round to the back of the residency – wonderful gardens, but there is that sheer drop to the sea which gives Benni goose pimples at the very thought of it.

No head for heights, that's my problem.

In the worst of the Troubles the military had forced prisoners to line up along the stone parapet, then they bayoneted them into the sea below. Women too, and kids. But that was all a long time ago, before Benni was old enough to become the eyes and ears of the island's occupying forces.

After all, spying pays better than begging: there's his autocycle to prove it; and the new Levi's Sister Osario is shortening for him.

She knows Benni is a spy; she knows he reports on her. Somehow she is fond of him all the same. Old people are crazy.

The pockets of his current trousers – a baggy pair of army issue stolen from a clothes line at the barracks – are, at the moment Colonel Fario enters the room, stuffed with cigars, petty cash from a drawer in the desk and a pen-set, a special gift to the colonel, commander of security operations on the island, from the president himself, with an inscription acknowledging 'services to the empire'.

This time Benni has been lucky. He has ducked into the knee-space of the colonel's vast mahogany desk. The colonel ushers into the room a young officer. 'Welcome to the island, Lieutenant.'

'Thank you, sir.'

Benni prays that there will be enough leg-room to accommodate the colonel and an undersized fourteen-year-old without their coming into too much contact with each other.

'You will appreciate, of course, that this conversation has never taken place.'

'I understand, sir.'

Benni is more silent than a mouse. He knows that Fario will have him shot for this second act of gross disobedience; and what he is about to overhear will extinguish any lingering chance of mercy.

'We do not call it murder, Lieutenant Gani,' the colonel is saying as the door to his office is firmly shut. 'We do not call it execution. Let us say, "Killed by an unknown hand". You are prepared?'

'I am honoured to have been selected, sir.'

Benni remembers this young man: stuck up, just in from Jakarta. His dad's somebody big. Benni got told off for being cheeky to the lieutenant.

Colonel Fario is offering Johannes Gani a very special mission. 'There are few whom we can trust, Johannes. To keep their mouth shut at all times – you understand that?'

'I must tell no one on pain of my own death.'

'Not even your father the general.' Colonel Fario turns towards the tall, elegant windows which overlook the island harbour. 'Nor should your commanding officer in the field, Captain Selim, know of your mission. He is a good man, with many scalps to his belt, though his weakness for native women has got him into trouble a little too often. It has cost him his promotion.'

Benni thinks, You can say that again, Colonel: Selim is the nutter of all nutters.

'You will find that the captain has his hands full protecting the Yellow Giants.'

'Yellow Giants, sir?'

'The earthmovers, brought in by the timber companies. It's my ambition that one day this island will be free of trees. Then we'll be able to plant sensible crops. Grow prosperous.'

4

'This Greenboots must be a very dangerous person, sir.'

'Please do not use that name. It is popular among the forest tribes. To us, he is trash, not a hero. Herr Mueller is an intruder on this island. A dirty German. He professes to study backward peoples. And believe me, the forest folk are backward. His books about them and the way we treat the islanders are a pack of lies.

'The order from the highest authority is – he must be silenced.'

Colonel Fario has pulled his chair up to the desk. His knees are close enough for Benni to scratch them. Even in the dark Benni notices Fario's trouser creases are sharp as knife blades.

'Before the United Nations delegation arrives, sir?'

'Exactly. By his writings, his broadcasts and his films Mueller has made the cause of the forest people famous. Thanks to him, the eyes of the world are on us: our human rights record is to be inspected.'

Lieutenant Johannes Gani, fresh from his commando training with the elite Kopassus fighters, receives his instructions. 'Should anything go wrong, we will disown you. Succeed in your mission and I can promise you a bright future.'

'Thank you, sir.'

Colonel Fario has lit a cigar. He does not offer one to Lieutenant Gani and he does not think to offer one to his other guest, Benni with an 'i'. He seems not to have noticed that there are only two cigars left in the box. He is pointing across the harbour. 'Do you know what is out there, soldier?'

Gani notes deep blue sea and the dark outlines of islands.

'Oil, in great abundance. That is why we can never give these people the independence they demand; and die for in their hundreds. In any event, we cannot grant independence here, for soon every idiot island and coon colony in the empire would want to be free.'

Colonel Fario now reaches across the mahogany desk to a pile of books. His shoe brushes against Benni's ankle. 'You will need to have read this, one of Mueller's lie machines, *Murder of a People*. A bestseller in the West, banned, of course, here.

'You must know it by heart – digest a few of his accusations. Learn a few names of massacres. Be sure you know all about the killings at Santa Cruz and the twenty-eight deaths at St Anthony's Rock.'

Four hundred, actually, remarks Benni to himself. My cousin was one of them.

Unaware of being contradicted, the colonel goes on, 'You will win Mueller's confidence by appearing to sympathize with the cause of the islanders. In short, fool him.'

The danger of Fario stepping on Benni and learning that a loudmouth kid knows of the authorities' plan to assassinate the hero of the forest folk, Hans Mueller, called Greenboots, momentarily passes. The colonel stands, moves round the desk, pours one glass of wine from a decanter

6

on a silver tray. He raises the glass towards the twenty-year-old lieutenant. 'Whatever the outcome of your enterprise, Johannes, it must remain an absolute secret. And for ever, understand?'

'For ever, sir.'

Benni thinks, for ever? I'll not be able to hold my tongue for twenty minutes. His confidence is growing. He will be back on his autocycle before the day is out.

Colonel Fario concludes, 'Our empire, young man, could, in the twenty-first century, be the most powerful in the world. The Americans know that, the British, the Chinese, that's why they support us – but only if the empire can hold together: One Nation, One People.'

'Absolutely, sir!'

'Then go and silence the singing canary, and serve your nation!'

'I will, sir. Thank you.' Gani is at the door. He hesitates. 'Sir?' He is puzzled. 'When I arrived here and walked into the town, people made this strange hissing sound as I passed. Like, "Shananaa" . . . What does it mean?'

Colonel Fario gulps down his wine and almost smashes the glass on the silver tray. 'You misheard –'

'No, "Shananaa", I specially –'

'You misheard – do you read me?'

'Yes, sir.' The shocked lieutenant retreats.

'And Gani, remember –'

'Sir?'

'There must be no witnesses. And no body.'

7

Colonel Fario has poured himself a second glass. There is one final reminder for Lieutenant Johannes Gani, assassin. 'Beware of the forest folk. They bewitched Hans Mueller and they may try their evil magic on you.'

Benni with an 'i' has the last – silent – word: 'Too true!'

1

ORDERS TO QUIT

Great Island, early morning
The trees are coming down. The sky, Muyu Father
had said, will soon be full of holes. The trees are
coming down and Muyu is dragging the leg that
is wounded. Where the bullet entered above the
knee the dark flesh has risen up, lost all its
smoothness, become like the bark of the trees. The
undergrowth protected him, but he had got too
close.

His friend Lyana had warned him. She waits
for him now, where the forest shuts out the sun.
She holds out a hand. She will be Muyu's strength
in the days to come. 'No good, you cannot stop
them. No one can.'

'My father – I cannot see him.'

She guides him away from looking.

'And Hans!'

'There is nothing you can do now. It is all over.'
In their eyes, the forest weeps. 'Come away!'

Great Island, seven days earlier
Here where the tribe once lived in unruffled
peace, there has always been twilight. It has been
enough; or at least, as the elders told the young

ones in their stories, enough for two thousand entrances to the world of Mother Forest. These trees knew the spirits when they were young. They protected them until the men from beyond the sea came with murder in their hands.

The machines are yellow like the morning sun. At first Muyu's people thought them gods. They glowed, they glistened, they roared. No forest ears had ever heard such sounds. Not even the gunfire of the soldiers from the Distant Masters could match them.

They are called, by Muyu's people, the Yellow Giants. Their faces scowl, never smile; and there is nothing that can resist their advance. Only the sawing, the never-ending sawing, only the swish of the trees, the crack of trunks compete with the voices of the Yellow Giants.

When the Yellow Giants first entered the forest, destroying the silence of the valleys, Muyu, aged fifteen, only child of Muyu Father, had believed, 'They will stay in the valley. The mountain slopes are too steep for them.'

Lyana, two years older than Muyu, was not of the tribe; she had known life in the towns, the ways of men from across the sea. She had known pain at their hands, and an injury she would never forget. 'Wherever there are trees, they will come. And when there are no trees they will come.'

Muyu had failed to understand. He waited.

'For they will bring settlers. From all the other islands, from the cities.'

'And the forest people?'

Lyana turned towards the distant roar of the Yellow Giants. 'You must ask Hans when he returns.'

'He will tell us to fight, perhaps.'

Lyana had stared into past time. You defend the trees with your arrows, and what then? The slaves of the Yellow Giants laugh and call for the soldiers; and the soldiers laugh for they are not afraid of bows and arrows.

'You must unite,' Hans Mueller, known as Greenboots, had urged his forest friends. 'There is no other way.'

It had been a mystery how Hans, the man with white skin and a dark beard, came among Muyu's people; with a pack on his back, in jeans, a T-shirt bearing on the front the design of a blue whale. Short, almost as short as the forest folk, and smoking a pipe, he wore the green Doc Martens which had earned his nickname among the tribes.

Muyu's father, headman or *suco* of the tribe, welcomed Hans to the village; a quiet place, twenty huts at most with open walls and thatched roofs. Greenboots brought with him a camera, tape recorder and many fat notebooks wrapped for protection in plastic shopping bags.

All he had said was, 'Tell me your stories.' He had lived among Muyu Father's people for over three years. One day he had returned from the Sad Place, the village beside the river, with a book. 'My words,' he had announced, 'and your lives: on record!'

'Record?'

'Well, a history that people all over the world can read.'

With a wry smile, Muyu Father asked, 'Is that good?'

'Of course, Muyu Father. It means that the cause of the forest people is known beyond the islands.' Hans flicked through the pages. 'See – pictures, of all the tribe. There's you, Chief. And Muyu. That's Lyana holding up a newborn piglet. There are the elders round the night fire.'

Hans closed the book, sighed, for two of the elders in the picture were dead. Lamely, he added, 'That's photography for you. Helps you remember.'

Muyu Father lowered his eyes. 'We remember.'

Yet Greenboots was too proud of his creation to leave the matter there. He grinned. 'In short, you're . . .' He paused, glanced at Lyana, whom he had taught German and English. 'Do the tribes have a word for "famous", Lyana?'

'Why?'

Greenboots laughed. Lyana was always one step ahead of him. 'Forgive me, Muyu Father. But you see, when an author gets published, the sky spirits rush to his head.'

Then, the Yellow Giants seemed far off.

A few days before their arrival, Hans journeyed alone beyond Soul Mountain to record the evidence of survivors of a tribe which had been attacked by government soldiers, a troop of Kopassus, the merciless ones. The elders were shot; the womenfolk raped, then beaten with gun butts; the young men taken to the capital for questioning.

None had been heard of since. Even if they had been free to return they would not have recognized their homeland; for it had been stripped bare by the Yellow Giants.

At the village of Muyu Father a man called Marquez came from the timber company, escorted by two soldiers.

He held up sheets of paper to Muyu Father. 'It is all agreed with your people. This is the signed document.'

Muyu Father took the paper, held it at arm's length as if it were a poisonous insect. Marquez turned it round. 'You've got it upside down, stupid.' He knew a little of the language of the forest people. 'It is an Order in Council. It requires you to vacate this village.'

'Vacate?'

'Move. Remove yourselves. Within seven days – you understand?'

'How is this? Our people have lived here since Great Island rose from the sea.'

'Not any longer.' Marquez had more to say. 'In any case, your people have no claim to the land. And it is not true you have occupied this village for a long time. In fact you people are wanderers, you build a village and then when it gets stiff with shit, you move on, leaving a mass of litter in the forest.'

Muyu Father retorted, 'All the forest is the Mother's gift to us, so long as we cherish it. We move our villages to let the leaves grow once more. Mother Forest gathers back what belongs to it. Always.'

Marquez was not happy to be dealing with a tribesman who was also a philosopher. 'The forest belongs to the government, Chief, and the government decides what to do with the forest.'

Lyana heard these words in torment. Hers was not the right to speak, but nothing could suppress her thoughts: it is you who have no rights. This island is not yours. You stole it from us, with your guns and your aeroplanes. It will never be yours even though you fill the valleys and the mountains with your battalions; even though you kill every one of us as you killed my family and all my clan.

Muyu Father rarely showed anger. Sometimes by his calmness he made Lyana angry. 'And the forest,' he had retorted, 'what has the forest decided?'

Marquez paused. 'You talk as if the forest had a mind of its own.'

'It has a mind. It has a soul. If you listen, you hear the heartbeat of the forest.'

'As far as I'm concerned, friend, this forest is a goddam nuisance. It's full of flies and lizards and snakes – and people like you who get in the way of progress. When I look at this forest, Chief, I see timber. I see sawmills. And I see things being made for the good of humanity. Timber for homes, timber for furniture, timber for building boats.'

'Oh yes,' Muyu Father replied. 'Some trees must fall. Some must be used, yes. We agree –'

'Listen, I don't want to be preached to on conservation by natives. This forest has fifty years of timbering in front of it. Anyway, the government has issued licences. And those licences mean one thing to your people – move on!'

All the villagers heard these words. As one voice they asked, 'Where do we move?'

'Further into the forest. There are thousands of kilometres of it not yet turned to timber.'

Marquez hated the forest and thus he did not begin to understand it. Muyu Father said, 'Sir, the forest is not like a long road. Everywhere is its centre, like the circles of the moon.'

Marquez was hot. The sweat made his feet squelch in his shoes. His shirt was dripping into his trousers and his trousers stuck to his legs as if his body fluids had turned to glue. 'The government knows what is best for you, my friend.'

'How can it know, when it is so distant, and when it does not listen?'

'It's you who should be doing the listening, Chief. Then you'll see sense. You'll go to the special villages built for you; send your children to school to be educated. To be frank, you people need civilizing. This is the twentieth century –'

'And your people, sir,' interrupted Muyu Father, 'you talk with guns. Yours is the justice of the dagger. You have brought massacre. Our people lie dead in the forest –'

'Because your people rose up against the government,' stormed back Marquez. 'Attacked the camps of the soldiers. And because you listened to the Resistance who would stir you up in hatred against the government.'

'We do not listen to the Resistance,' returned Muyu Father.

'That is what you say. Soldiers who stray in the bush, they die. Not because of the snakes, but because your people obey the rebels, do their dirty work while they vanish in the forest to start new troubles elsewhere.'

'We do not listen to the Resistance,' repeated Muyu Father, glancing at his son. Muyu nodded, though reluctantly; and his gaze met Lyana's: her elder brother had joined the resistance movement. They caught him. Tortured him. Gave him a ride in a helicopter; and over the sea, invited him to 'take a walk'; as the soldiers put it, *mandi laut* – gone for a swim.

Marquez knew he was wasting his time and his breath; yet he had one more accusation to make. 'Also, you listen to the Bearded One, the so-called Greenboots – do you deny that?'

Muyu Father shrugged. 'The Bearded One lives among us. That is all. He is not of the Resistance.'

'Maybe not. I'm surprised he's not here now trying to block us with his lawyer's claptrap.' In fact Marquez was relieved not to have to confront Greenboots. Things would be much easier without the interloper reading out the Universal Declaration of Human Rights on behalf of his adopted friends.

Time for action. 'No more arguments, Chief. I have orders. The Yellow Giants come in seven days, one hour after dawn. Take all your property with you.'

'Property?' The word, like 'famous', has no parallel in any of the many tongues of the forest people.

'Belongings – your pigs, man, and your bows and arrows, though if I had my way I'd have them confiscated.'

There was a waiting as the two men glared at each other. And the forest whispered in a new wind from the south.

'Come on,' said Marquez, as Muyu Father stood still as a hunter aiming at his prey. 'Give me your word. I don't want any trouble.'

Marquez momentarily glanced over his shoulder as if Captain Selim, a man he feared as much as the forest people did, was already ordering his men into battle formation.

'What I want, Chief, is empty huts. You will not yet have made the acquaintance of Captain Selim, but I imagine his reputation will have already reached you. Do not cross him. Obey him to the letter – quit this place without fuss – and you will survive.

'Seven days, Chief. Very generous in the circumstances. Then we shall be coming in for a dawn start.' Marquez fixed his gaze upon Muyu, sensing the youth's hidden rage. 'And with machine-guns ready for any hot-heads who protest.'

For a second the eyes of Lyana held Marquez' stare. She is a beauty, he thought, but that look alone could cut a man's throat. He was tempted to warn Muyu Father – keep the girl out of sight of Selim. Instead, he wagged his finger and repeated, 'Empty huts, Chief!'

2

MOTHER FOREST MUST DECIDE

The same evening the elders of the tribe met in parley. The forest was unusually tranquil. The south wind had dropped. It was as if the trees around them as they argued matters in Muyu Father's hut had already, in spirit, departed.

Muyu and Lyana sat among them, her arm around his waist, his across her shoulders. This closeness gave Muyu comfort for he was afraid of the future. The forest had given his tribe life from the beginning of the earth; yet now the forest was to be taken away from them.

Lyana too was afraid. She stared into the bright eye of the fire, at the rays of heat which turned the forest into slow-dancing spirits. At last among these people she had known safety and love.

Twice already Muyu Father's people had been moved on. Twice they had seen no alternative. The government says: that had been the command. The soldiers made sure it was obeyed.

But Hans had come among them since the last time the village was cleared. He was back now from his trip over the mountain. He brought news: 'There is to be a visit to Great Island – people from the United Nations. A delegation to investigate abuses of human rights.'

He paused, peered across the woodsmoke at his companions, puffed on his pipe. He was deeply upset by his visit to the village beyond Soul Mountain. 'I shall go to the capital, Muyu Father. Report to the delegation on what is happening here.'

He caught Lyana's smile which seemed to say, Tell us something new. Hans nodded; but he was ever the optimist. 'Okay, the delegation will speak some fine words on the liberty of the people, then they will retire to the governor's residence for roast pheasant and champagne.

'But look at it this way, there will be the chance to talk to journalists, spread the news about the army's plan to exterminate us, village by village, tribe by tribe.'

Muyu Father rested his chin on cupped hands. 'You have told our story to the peoples beyond the ocean, yes?'

Hans glowed; as well as being an optimist, he was an egotist, proud of the stir he had made worldwide on behalf of his adopted people.

'Yet,' went on Muyu Father, gently, 'the more our story is known, the more the Distant Masters are angry with us; the more the soldiers come to murder our people.'

Greenboots tugged at his beard, uneasy. True, the more publicity Hans had won for the plight of Muyu's people, the more stories that appeared in foreign newspapers and on television concerning the destruction of the forest, the herding of the tribes into camps with high fences, the more reports there were of new diseases bringing down the forest people, the more angry the government had become.

'All things have become worse with us,' Muyu Father continued.

'Would things have been better for you, Muyu Father, if I had never opened my mouth?'

The forest and the elders were silent. For the tribe, silence is a bar to quarrelling. There would be no answer either way and Hans Mueller knew this. He turned to Lyana for support. She alone of the tribe could read; she alone was familiar with Hans' work, his ideas. Her mind alone reached beyond these island shores.

Yet she too honoured the silence. Did they not all feel the same, that soon there would be the silencing of the forest?

Muyu Father eased the pressure on his friend by changing the subject. 'While you were away, you had a visitor – a young soldier.'

Now Lyana broke her silence. 'He had your book.'

'A soldier with my book? Impossible!'

Lyana had found the young officer handsome; different from the other soldiers she had met. 'He wished to talk to you.'

Lieutenant Johannes Gani had come to the village alone. He said he was under the command of Captain Selim, the mention of whose name made Lyana shudder. 'I wish to warn you,' he had said to Muyu Father. 'The captain has a reputation. To avoid bloodshed, please obey him. Do not question his orders.'

Gani was disappointed not to have met the famous Greenboots. He had taken out a copy of Hans' book, its cover half torn off, pages curled and rain-soaked; and he had said, 'This book has made many converts back home in Java. Herr Mueller is very convincing in his argument for the independence of Great Island.'

Gani had put his finger to his lips, smiled. 'If Captain Selim heard me say such a thing he would have me court-martialled.' He had stared at Lyana as all visitors did. He had eyed Muyu, classified him as a probable threat, a young leopard awaiting his moment to leap. He had counted the villagers; seen no evidence of real arms.

Reporting to his captain, Gani had said, 'They will give no trouble, sir.'

'And Greenboots?' asked Captain Selim. Short yet lithe, Selim took special pride in his Ray-ban sunglasses. He was polishing their lenses now, permitting a rare glimpse of his piercing gaze. Tiger's eyes, Gani decided.

'Greenboots is due back in the village. It's my view he will caution people against taking action.'

Selim stared at the young lieutenant. He had already figured him: a young toff from the capital; dad high up in command; three months in the jungle and he will be promoted and welcomed back home with a medal and a new posting to somewhere swish like Bali; leaving the likes of Captain Selim to soldier on in sweat and filth.

'And how have you come to this conclusion,

Lieutenant – by reading the mind of the enemy in his absence?'

'Easy, sir – by reading his book. Greenboots writes that violence serves no purpose. He is a pacifist.'

'I could put you on a charge for reading such a book.' Captain Selim replaced his Ray-bans. Lieutenant Gani lowered his head. 'However, as I have read it myself – and find it to be trash – I shall overlook your indiscretion.'

'Thank you, sir.'

Selim lit a cigar. 'You college boys, Lieutenant, have a lot to learn about the real world. Take my word for it, faced with the Yellow Giants, those coolies will fight.'

'Bows and arrows against guns? Can they be that stupid, Captain?'

Selim squashed a mosquito on the back of his hand. 'In this forest, it is not always possible to prove who fires first.'

'You mean –?' Gani did not finish his question. He waited, confused, wondering whether he, now, was the stupid one.

'What do I mean, Lieutenant?'

'But your orders, sir: you told the men – the less bloodshed, the better.'

The captain sucked irritably on his cigar. 'Oh yes – my orders!'

Never until recent days had Muyu Father given the slightest hint that his own ideas had begun to change. But such a hint coloured his words now.

'We have bows and arrows. The soldiers have guns. Even if we had guns, the soldiers would bring more and more soldiers and more guns.

'And yet . . .'

His words faltered: in all his life he had known few enemies, and these he had encountered only in ceremonial battles that usually ended in word-plays and feasting.

Muyu was encouraged by his father's doubts. He was remembering what Hans had told them about the village he had visited: the people had not resisted, yet they had been punished all the same. Muyu said, 'We have the forest on our side, Father. We know its secret paths. In the forest, we see the soldiers but they do not see us. They look and they see only the lizard's eye and the snake's tail.'

The elders were impressed, except Muyu Father. 'And still the soldiers win,' he said. 'And still the Yellow Giants eat up the forest.'

Hans Mueller held Muyu Father in great respect yet marvelled at his innocence. 'It is true, Chief, that where the tribes have fought back, they have often lost the battle, but they have not lost the argument.'

From Muyu Father, a smile, full of ancient wisdom. He held Greenboots in great respect, yet marvelled at his innocence. His head shook slowly, first showing one cheek to the light of the fire, then the other.

'You people of the West, you speak of arguments as if they might put food into our mouths, protect our huts against the great storms. Yet the soldiers do not fire arguments from their guns.'

Hans had not finished his case. 'The tribes have lost, Muyu Father, because they have failed to hold hands in unity. Only when all the forest people join together will there be victory.'

'Yet you counselled us not to fight.'

'My views are changing. The Yellow Giants will not yield to persuasion, I am afraid. But fighting alone – that is not the way.' Hans nodded at each elder in turn, convinced he was making progress. 'You see, our hope has got to be with the Resistance. We must not believe the army when they say the resistance fighters are all dead or captured.'

Hans' pipe needed relighting. He reached towards the fire and used a burning twig. 'Yet, Chief, you do not support the Resistance even though they too wish to drive out the soldiers and the Yellow Giants once and for all. When their representatives come to the village you disappear into the trees. Why is that?'

Muyu Father stared through the firesmoke into the dark thoughts of the forest. 'Those who would set our country free will also bring with them their ideas. It is written on their foreheads – things must be different. They will ask us the same questions – why do we not wish for change, for a better life? And we will have to answer: there is no better life.'

'I am afraid,' replied Hans in a voice trembling a little as the leaves above him, 'that you wish for the one thing which is impossible.'

Muyu Father laughed. 'We ask for nothing – yet you say that is impossible?'

Hans tapped his pipe against his boot and refilled the bowl with fresh tobacco. 'Out in the ocean, Chief, the West is drilling for oil. Farewell the fishermen. Here you are sitting on a fortune in the world's best timber. Somewhere in Geneva or London there's a housewife impatiently waiting for her new wood-panelled kitchen. Is the government to deny her?'

Muyu Father stretched out his forefinger as if it were a pen. 'I am sure, Hans, that if you write to her one of your wonderful letters, she will understand . . .'

The debate was to end as it always did, with an agreement to differ. 'At least assure me of this, Chief, that until we have bullets to answer bullets – no arrows!'

Greenboots now explored the faces of all his listeners, finally those of Lyana and Muyu. He too saw in Muyu the young leopard about to spring. 'Right? Hm, I see another tale written in your face, my young friend.' He turned to Lyana. 'Is there a word for "heroics" in the languages of the tribes?'

' "Madness"?' suggested Lyana.

'Not exactly.' Hans watched Muyu lean towards the fire, adding a dry log to its fierce heart. The burning wood spat into the night.

No one spoke. No one moved. Eyes shut on their own thoughts. All at once Hans Mueller sensed – they have decided. The cold night which lay across his back swept into his limbs and he felt terror, for himself and for all of the tribe.

He had only Lyana to appeal to, for she alone had witnessed the slaughter of her own people. 'Tell them, Lyana – remind them. To raise one hand against the soldiers at this time ... Tell them!'

Lyana's gaze crossed the firelight and the faces. 'They know my story.'

Hans felt alone as never before in his life: from belonging here, he had become the outsider.

Now Muyu Father bent forward. He placed his hand over that of Greenboots. 'We have no plans, my friend, to fight or not to fight. We shall answer what is in our hearts when the time comes. Mother Forest will speak. She will advise us.'

Somewhere deep in the forest an owl swooped for its supper. In the silence, the villagers heard the brief screech of the helpless victim. Greenboots sighed. For him, Mother Forest had spoken.

3

No Unnecessary Bloodshed

Muyu stirs to the sound of the Yellow Giants. They have advanced long before dawn. They have not kept their word: do they ever? And now they are waiting beside the first huts.

The forest is clad in mist; cold drops of overnight rain splash from leaf to leaf as if measuring the seconds till morning. The villagers appear not to have stirred, not to have planned the next step of their lives. Only Hans Mueller shows himself, strides towards the Yellow Giants, faces Marquez where the slope into the village is steepest.

'No pictures!' Marquez has insisted. Behind him, and between the Yellow Giants, are soldiers – thirty of them – with weapons raised. Their commander, Captain Selim, keeps his distance at the edge of the forest clearing. He is accompanied by his second-in-command, Lieutenant Johannes Gani.

'Why no photographs if all this is legal, Señor Marquez?'

'No pictures.'

'Parley, then?'

'We have spoken enough. This village comes down. The whole of the area must be felled during the next six days.'

'And if we resist?'

'Get back to where you belong, Herr Mueller – and take your fine ideas and your green boots with you.'

'You will shoot me – a westerner?'

'No. But Captain Selim surely will. He scares me and I reckon he ought to terrify you and your friends.'

Selim's exploits are well known to Hans. Among the forest folk he is known as the Butcher with the Black Eyes. 'Then we are to be made an example?'

Marquez fears for his own safety. 'Listen, I have a job to do, but I want no trouble. No bloodshed – so tell your mates.'

The mist which stretches across the village and hovers among the trees at the forest edge now clears a fraction to reveal the warriors of the tribe, faces and bodies painted, some wearing head-dresses; all of them with knives at their sides, bows in their hands.

Marquez gasps. 'So they mean to fight?'

Hans Mueller shakes his head. 'It is a ceremony – a tradition. This is how the forest people of old solved their differences. By display of war. Not war itself.'

'They're armed – that's all I know.'

'Let me speak to Selim, explain.'

'What'll they do – a war dance?'

'They will advance towards you, make the gestures of war. Then they will retire into the forest.'

Marquez turns, calls to Captain Selim. 'You know about this, Captain?'

Selim advances. He is not listening. 'Advise them to lay down their bows, Marquez. You, Herr Mueller, are under arrest.'

'Hang on.' Marquez remembers his own instructions from the company: no unnecessary violence. Bad for the company image; and he knows Selim is under instruction to avoid provocation. Arresting Greenboots will provoke retaliation.

He tries to be reasonable. 'If it means they'll go quietly,' said Marquez, 'maybe we should let them do their war dance. Would you stand surety, Mueller?'

'I'm under arrest, it seems.'

Marquez speaks up for Hans Mueller. 'There's no warrant for his arrest, Captain. I mean –'

'Forget what you mean, Marquez, and listen to what *I* mean: no dancing. Tell them, Greenboots – lay down their weapons and we shall take no further action against them.'

Muyu Father now approaches from between the huts. He wears the head-dress of the chief of the tribe. He is proudly painted, only the blue-white lines on his face tell a modern, not an ancient story: they take the form of the anti-nuclear symbol.

'A piece of your artwork, is it, Mueller?' asks Selim. 'I could arrest him and have him flogged just for that.'

Marquez taps his watch. 'For heaven's sake,

Captain, let them have their war dance, or we'll be jaw-jawing all morning.'

'No dance.' Selim strides towards Muyu Father. 'And I want that paint off your face, Daddy-o.'

Hans Mueller steps between Selim and Muyu Father. His own hand goes up to deflect Selim's which, in another moment, would have smudged the offensive image that seems to mock him.

The soldier accompanying Captain Selim sees his commander outnumbered, one against two. He calls for support, moves forward. Greenboots has been pushed aside yet struggles to remain a buffer between Selim and the chief.

At the rim of the forest Muyu has strung an arrow to his bow. Though he will eventually be blamed, his decision to act is not wilful or wild. Muyu Father is being attacked. Greenboots is being pistol-whipped by the officer.

Muyu's arrow crosses the village clearing. Its flight is witnessed by the other warriors of the tribe, though it is unseen by the enemy. The soldier beside Captain Selim is pierced through the neck.

The short battle of the high forest has begun.

Selim leaves the soldier where he fell. He fears arrows, and arrows pursue him, though none strikes him. Once clear, he issues a command to fire. First to die is the silence of the forest. Birds rise in terrified clouds above the roof of trees.

Lyana watches from a screen of bushes on higher ground. She has quarrelled with Muyu. He

31

has turned his back on her. 'You will fight, yes? And you will die. That is stupid.'

Muyu loves Lyana, so her words hurt him to the heart. He had grunted, waved her out of his sight. 'Go with the other women, then!'

He had wanted to turn, call her again, but his pride was stronger than sense. He had closed his eyes and when he looked again the mist had drawn her into its shadow.

Muyu has the strength around him of the other boys of the tribe. The son of their chief has led the way. They too have grown tired of the ways of the elders.

They too say – enough!

Hurt that Lyana does not understand the ways of a warrior, Muyu forgets her in the thrill of battle. As son of the chief he has much to prove. I am to be a man this day. He, perhaps he alone, a voice from a dream tells him, can defeat the Yellow Giants; and the tribe will then sing his name in praise till the ending of the world.

Still, Lyana's voice haunts him: 'Your arrows will only bring sorrow!'

He had replied, cruelly, 'You are not of our people, so you will not understand.'

He has killed a man. And the soldiers have also taken life. The forest shakes with the noise of the Yellow Giants, trailing blue spumes of smoke as they advance across the village clearing.

Hans Mueller has thrown himself on the ground. He hears shots above and around him. He hears death. Another soldier falls, topples from the front of a Yellow Giant and is crushed beneath its metal feet.

Marquez screams, in fear, disgust, awe. So far in his life he has managed to avoid killing. He is not among those who slaughter for pleasure. Now that it has happened his one thought is to lay the blame on someone else. 'The boy started it!' And it is Muyu, nearest to the forest edge, who will always be framed in Marquez' vision as the boy who altered the lives of everyone present, and for ever.

The younger boys have retreated into the bush. Only Muyu and his friend Dani hold their ground. Marquez points, yells, 'The boy! Get him.' Already on his lips are the words Marquez intends to use to explain these events to his employers: 'It was the natives, not us, who started it. We came in peace.'

Where Muyu had been standing a second ago, tree bark is ripped open by the spray of machine-gun fire from the armoured vehicle which has swung into action from across the village.

Dani is hit. He is carried back into the shadow of the forest. He is coughing blood. Muyu abandons his last arrows. He stoops towards Dani, takes his hand, tries to lift him; yet the gunfire of the soldiers is concentrated here.

Like the touch of a white-hot stone a single bullet enters the back of Muyu's thigh, passes out through flesh and hits Dani in the chest. He falls back, eyes already signalling the end of him, which is the end of the battle, the end of the tribe.

Muyu tries to lift Dani on to his shoulder. Yet he knows the pointlessness of it. He lays his friend down and suddenly the searing agony of his leg forces him to abandon all thought of moving, of escaping.

He is on the ground. The machine-gun has finished speaking. Now the soldiers are coming for him, firing as they advance.

Muyu begins to crawl. His head is a storm of confusion. The forest is drawing him inwards, whispering, 'Here, this way!' and the voices multiply: Which way? This way. No, this. Run. Can't run. They will catch you if you walk.

Cut off your head if you crawl.

Captain Selim has anticipated the whispers of the forest. 'Bring the boy's head!' It is proof; and heads are easier to carry than corpses. They can be decorative. And they are good for reminding these people who is boss.

Without help, Muyu is lost. The pain has extinguished his strength, his sense of direction, his will to escape. Everything has gone wrong. Nothing can ever be put right. Let them take you. And when they take you, there will be some more pain. And then, nothing. I shall be like Dani.

All at once the dark avenues of the forest are speckled with the flash of fruit bats' wings and these, together, create a sound almost like the approach of the Yellow Giants.

Muyu falls, climbs half to his feet, staggers a few paces, then falls again. He is angry at himself and out of anger grows a little strength. He rises, walks, almost trots. His wound will have to be tied off. The blood is bubbling like a red stew.

His head is a dream again. The fruit bats are eating his brain. How did they get in there? Soon there will be room enough for snakes. They will coil and coil and they will lay their young who will coil and coil and lay their own young.

From the dark bush beside him, a shadow. He has strength enough to draw his knife; yet the bats have not eaten so much of his brain that he fails to recognize Lyana.

She takes his arm, bears his weight, says nothing. 'My leg!' These are tears to mix with his blood. 'Lyana . . .'

His companion will say her piece in good time. For now, she rests him across her shoulders. She stands, sways, tests her strength and balance against Muyu's weight.

Lyana knows: the battle may be at an end, yet the pursuit is only beginning. She heads for the heart of Mother Forest.

4

GOLDEN GOOSE

Blades of sunlight stab the mist, turning it to silver steam, the last refuge of phantoms. The soldiers have found the boy whom Marquez claims started the battle. They have severed his head, brought it out into the forest clearing which is now shrouded with smoke.

The village huts have been burnt to the earth. Soldiers are dragging the bodies of the tribesmen to a pit dug by one of the Yellow Giants.

Captain Selim is filled with the spirit of the chase. Two soldiers have been killed, one by Muyu's arrow, the other by a stray bullet. 'I want the woods scoured centimetre by centimetre, Lieutenant Gani, till every one of this tribe pays for the deaths of my men.'

'Yes, sir.' Lieutenant Gani is shaking with what he has witnessed; the speed of it, the brutality of it. He has never seen men die like this. His own weapon remains unfired. 'And the prisoner?'

'He will await my justice.'

A soldier has brought in the head of Dani.

'Take it away,' pleads Marquez. 'God, he was just a kid.'

Selim commands Hans Mueller to be brought forward. Greenboots has been badly beaten. His

36

face is a mass of blood. One lens of his spectacles is shattered. His arms are bound behind his back. He is forced to kneel.

'You see what happens, Mueller, when you shove your nose into affairs that don't concern you?' Selim turns, surveys the scene of death and burning. 'This is your work. And be sure you will be held responsible. I'm going to see to it that your name is shit across the world.'

The captain points to the head of Dani. 'And that is the price the innocent pay for your meddling. Be it on your own conscience, Mr Greenboots.'

Selim waits. Hans' lips dribble blood. There is blood in his thinning hair. There is a gash down his neck. His shoulder is unnaturally hunched as if something is broken. 'Now tell me, Mueller, before I decide to shoot you through the eyes as I did the insolent chief of this tribe – is this the boy chief, the son of the *suco*?'

Marquez glances at Lieutenant Gani: both of them know that this is not Muyu. Marquez is sick of the whole business. He guesses easily enough what will happen if Selim is not convinced he has captured the son of the headman. He will hunt the forest till he has killed every youth of the same age.

Just as King Herod did in the land of Palestine, fearful of the godly child who might rob him of his throne.

Marquez will say nothing.

'Speak, Mueller. Is this the boy chief or isn't it?'

Greenboots shakes his head and the agony of it makes him cry out. 'If I say no, will you believe me? If I say yes, will you believe me?'

Lieutenant Johannes Gani has his secret orders. He is pondering the advantage of keeping silent or confirming that this is not the head of Muyu.

He agrees, Greenboots must die, but not as a martyr; for then his murder would be reported in newspaper headlines in every country on earth. Gani senses that he hears the words of Colonel Fario: 'Mueller must disappear in the forest without trace.'

Yet Captain Selim appears to have every intention of sparing the life of Hans Mueller. 'You still have your wits about you, I see, Greenboots.' He is nodding. 'So I shall tell you the plans I have for both of us. You . . . are my little golden goose, my passport out of this stinking jungle. And do you know what, together we're going to be celebrities with our mugs on TV. How about that?'

Gani is breathless with a new fear, that Selim will ruin Colonel Fario's plans for the slaying of Greenboots. He calculates: If I'm left in charge of the prisoner while Selim goes hot-foot after Muyu and the other tribesmen, then my mission could be back on course.

Over-eager, he interrupts his commanding officer. 'Sir, that isn't the youth called Muyu. He must have escaped into the forest.'

Marquez groans: these few words will turn his simple task of chopping down trees into a nightmare of attacks and reprisals.

He hates the military. They are arrogant. They are cruel. And they are stupid: they act only for the moment, never considering the future. 'Well it certainly looks like him to me, Captain. I mean, bearing in mind they all look alike . . .'

Gani is fighting to win the argument. 'There was a girl too, sir – called Lyana.'

'Ly . . .' Selim starts to repeat the name then halts, flicks it away from his consciousness as he would do a fly from his sleeve. Yet he remembers: something, vague as the mist clearing from the forest, enshrouding like the woodsmoke.

'A beauty,' adds Marquez.

Oh yes: now Selim remembers, but the uncertainty which leaps into his eyes is concealed by his proud Ray-bans. He edges away from the subject. 'There'll have been plenty of women and children, gone to the mountain. We'll ferret them out, don't worry.'

Selim seems to have lost the thread of his intentions. 'So there we have it.' He no longer, for the moment, seems interested whether this is the head of the boy chief or not. He is like a person in the grip of a dream, or troubling memories.

Johannes Gani takes his chance. 'If that dead boy really isn't the son of the chief, sir, and if the chief's son was the one who started this horrible affair, he must be captured. Brought to justice.'

Selim's thoughts are still far away. He is talking to his own doubts and anxieties when he says, aloud, yet to himself alone, 'There are plenty of Lyanas.' His attention returns to Hans Mueller

39

only to be interrupted once more by Lieutenant Gani:

'Permit me, sir, to suggest a patrol.'

Selim does not like Gani. He senses that the young officer thinks he knows better than his commander; that he is sharper, more intelligent. And Selim suspects that he is right. Gani will go far; much farther than this crude but courageous servant of his nation.

Unless, that is, Captain Selim suddenly becomes the hero of his people: captor of the infamous Greenboots. 'Permit me, Lieutenant,' responds Selim, 'to do the thinking around here and to give the orders. Are you listening?'

'Sir?'

'I want a smart wooden cage built for my golden goose. Nice and comfy, Greenboots, that's what you're going to be. When we get to the coast we'll both have our picture taken. The TV cameras will roll. Then we'll charge you with leading the tribes to insurrection and hang you like a common thief.'

Marquez raises his hand as if he were back in class. 'Captain, is it okay to get the machines moving?'

Selim nods. 'But first make sure our little treasure doesn't bleed to death. And I want his cage tough enough to hold King Kong.'

In broken sleep, Muyu grunts. The pain in his thigh is a lightless tunnel. He is sliding down it; a story of old is mixing in with his dark dreaming.

In the ancient days the elders of the tribe heard of a far-off country where there existed a wondrous truth. They dispatched a messenger along stream-filled caverns deep beneath the forest.

The traveller had emerged after many days and as he did so, stepping into the light for the first time, he discovered his skin was no longer brown. It was as the elders had prophesied. The man of white skin would bring back to the tribes the key to wisdom.

Yet instead of a saviour the man of white skin proved a false friend. The Portuguese and the Dutch had come from across the great ocean and conquered the island people. Then the men of yellow skin arrived: the Japanese, unleashing a typhoon of death. Finally came the worst invaders of all, the murderous Bapaks, the Indonesian conquerors.

Lyana has bound Muyu's wound with leaves and woven strings of grass. It is dusk now. The forest smells of burning carried on a fresh wind which has passed over the dead village. Muyu awakes, watches Lyana. She has put sticking plaster on a cut across his forehead; and there are more items she is using from Greenboots' rucksack.

'Where have you been, Lyana?' He is stunned at her nerve. 'They would've killed you.'

'They are drunk.' She fishes in Greenboots' rucksack. She manages a smile as she produces a tin of tobacco, a paper bag full of sweets, a small tin of concentrated milk and then, accompanied by a look of pride, Hans' precious log, bound in simulated leather.

'Is he dead?'

'He is hurt. They made a prison for him, a wooden trap. He has been out in the sun all day. I think he has little strength left. We must save him.'

Muyu knows he must now ask the question which will cause him the deepest, the most searing pain. 'And Muyu Father?'

Lyana drops her head in sorrow. 'All the warriors died. Tonight Mother Forest honours Muyu Father.' She touches Muyu's hand. 'The forest also cries out on behalf of the forest people.'

Muyu sighs. 'Two of us?'

'Didn't Muyu Father always say, each leaf that falls leaves its spirit on the branch for new leaves to grow?'

'And if the Yellow Giants destroy all the trees?'

'Then we shall destroy the Yellow Giants.'

'How?'

Lyana slings Greenboots' rucksack on to her shoulder. She takes Muyu's hand, gently eases him on to his feet. 'Now that you are chief, Muyu, it is you who should answer the questions.'

He is feeling better. He has eaten and rested. Lyana has now banished his gloom but she will not let it defeat him. He smiles for the first time. 'Perhaps I will!'

'So?'

'We go to the camp, yes?'

'If we don't, Greenboots will die.'

'And then, Lyana?'

Reassured that Muyu seems strong enough to make his own way, though limping, she says, 'Perhaps we must also look for a new life.'

'Away from the forest?'

She dares to entertain the thought. 'Perhaps.'

Muyu's mind is shut to such a possibility. 'Never!'

5

CONSPIRACY

In the night camp of the soldiers, Captain Selim is relaxed. An oil lamp lights his tent and the faces of his guests sitting in canvas chairs. Marquez is on his third glass of whisky yet remains broodingly silent. Lieutenant Gani is better company though he sips only occasionally at his glass as if afraid to have it topped up yet again.

'In the history books,' says Selim, 'they will name today's victory the Battle of the High Forest. The turning of the tide against the resistance of the tribes. Correct, Lieutenant?'

Gani's mind is fuddled with drink and worry: he has been to visit Greenboots in his cage. The man is dying. 'Correct, sir,' he replies without enthusiasm. In Gani's view, the great battle did not even warrant being called a skirmish.

'How many native warriors came through that forest, Marquez?'

Marquez has been wrestling all day with his conscience: should he complain to his superiors about Selim's brutality; and if he did, would they listen? Probably not: it would be a civilian's word against an officer's. 'About a dozen, Captain.'

'A dozen? Are you joking? Dozens! Probably a hundred, possibly more. They came at us from all sides. It is in my report to Command HQ. Only the discipline of my men stood between us and a massacre.'

Selim pours out more drink. 'Greenboots is no fool. He would never have ordered an attack unless he was convinced he had enough warriors to beat us. No fool! Correct, Gani?'

'No fool, sir.' This, muses the lieutenant, is how history gets written.

'So you agree with me about the numbers – both of you?'

'I didn't see no hundreds, Captain,' Marquez confesses.

'Of course you didn't – because of the mist, and then the smoke.'

'We were not supposed to burn their huts down, Captain,' persists Marquez.

Selim has been pleasant. The drink has made him so. Now he is turning nasty. The drink is making him so. 'You have a wife and four kids, correct, Marquez? They rely on your wages?' The captain glances out at the forest. 'And it's a long way home – many dangers.'

Marquez gets the message. 'True, Captain.'

'Now let's run through that again – how many warriors?'

Marquez is exhausted. He wants to go to bed. He wants to get out of this jungle. He wants to forget. 'Possibly a hundred?'

With Johannes Gani, college-educated, Captain Selim is more careful. 'If you were Greenboots, Lieutenant, and you had gathered the tribes for an attack, how many men would you reckon you needed – fifty, a hundred?'

Gani recognizes the trap Selim has laid for him: it is stupidly obvious. He tries argument. 'We've no real proof, sir, that Greenboots had anything to do with the attack. After all, he was waiting beside the village, unarmed.'

'That is not the question I asked you, Lieutenant. If you were Greenboots –'

'Yes, sir, I heard the question.'

'Well?'

'At least fifty, sir. Yet as I say –'

Selim cuts Gani off abruptly. 'That is all I want to know. Now go and inspect the prisoner. He was looking feverish the last time I saw him. We don't want him dying on our hands. He has a journey to make. And a triumphal entry into the capital with Captain Mohammed Selim receiving the blessings of a grateful nation.'

The captain raises his glass for the lamplight to shine through it. 'Dear me, is this little vessel empty already? More, Marquez?'

'Not for me, Captain.'

Marquez jolts back in his seat for he is staring down the barrel of Selim's revolver. 'When the captain – or shall we say colonel? – drinks, my friend, his guests also drink. Correct?'

'Right, Captain. '

'Colonel! And say "correct".'

'Right, Colonel – correct. Whatever you say.'

'And how many warriors were there, Marquez?'

46

'At least a hundred.'

'Bearing what weapons?'

'Bows and –'

'No, idiot!'

'Guns.'

'Now you're talking. Guns supplied by whom, Marquez?'

'The Resistance.'

Captain Selim is relaxed once more. He lights a cigar. 'The facts are what you make them: correct, Marquez?'

Marquez nods, drinks to settle his nerves. 'Correct . . . er, Colonel!'

In his cage, built so small he cannot stretch out his legs or stand, Greenboots is conscious, yet drugged – by the blows to his head, by the heat of the day which had turned sweat to a slime of blood and dry earth and now by the bitter cold.

He had lost consciousness in the afternoon. He was granted one good dream: he was sitting on a beach near Sydney. Long-time (and long-suffering) girlfriend Emily Bryson was curled up beside him, and saying, 'I think I'll join you in the forest after all. I'm sick of city life.'

'You've your career to think about.'

'Journalism's for youngsters with bags of energy. I'm over the hill and my energy's running out.'

'You've the stamina of a squirrel and you're a success.'

'You just say that so you can sally forth on one more expedition.'

'The book's almost finished.'

'You seem to be fonder of Muyu and his tribe and this mysterious Lyana than you are of me.'

'Let's not go over all that again.'

'Well, this time I'm coming to see what it's all about, your little paradise.'

Paradise? The word awakens Hans. Okay, Emily, come and see my paradise. Bring bandages, some aspirin.

'Will whisky do? The best in the world.'

Something he has been dearly looking forward to. That will do fine. He remembers the condition he is in. And you'd also better bring a spade to bury me.

From the tents fifty metres away, where the light is and where the hum of voices reminds Hans that his life here is over, someone is approaching. Hans has tried to engage the two guards in conversation. He needs water, food, but they are under orders to ignore him.

'Stand down for a moment – take a smoke.' The voice is that of Johannes Gani.

'Thank you, sir.'

'Aye, much obliged, Lieutenant.'

'Here, share that.' Gani offers them a can of Foster's. He has another. The moment the guards reach their comrades around a bonfire in the centre of the forest clearing, he presses the beer through the bars of Greenboots' cage.

48

'I'm sorry for the way you've been treated, Herr Mueller.'

Greenboots tugs at the ring-pull, drinks. He is dizzy. This is fever. It will get worse. He needs help, yet he cannot resist saying his piece:

'Being sorry, Lieutenant, won't bring back Muyu Father and his people.'

'I am sorry for that too. Believe me, I argued with the captain . . . There were other ways. Not in his book, however. He has become –'

'A monster?'

'I fear so.'

'What is to happen to me?' Greenboots asks.

Gani delays his reply. He looks around him, lowers his voice. 'I have . . . sympathies, Herr Mueller.'

'I'm not a "Herr" any more or even a "Mister". I'm a slave in a cage too small for a monkey. I won't last another day.'

'Unless, somehow, you were released. Could you make it through the forest?'

Greenboots is suspicious. 'Freed? Just who are you, Lieutenant? Selim would shoot you for even thinking such things.'

'Hans . . .' Gani pauses. 'You must trust me. I've read your book. I'm a member of a number of organizations which could at the very least earn me a reprimand.'

'If I disappear, you will be arrested.'

'But if we both disappeared?'

'You would desert?'

Gani draws his revolver from its leather holster.

'Let us say I became *your* prisoner.' He turns the handle of the pistol towards Greenboots.

'I've not the strength to cock the trigger, my friend.' Yet Greenboots is interested: the alternatives have no attraction.

'Then rest a while. I will summon the guards. And relieve them again in the middle of the night.'

'Are you Resistance, Lieutenant?'

'Johannes is my name.' Gani returns the revolver to its holster. He calls the guards, then swiftly seeks confirmation of Greenboots' assent to his plan. 'Okay, Hans?'

Greenboots hesitates, sensing desires struggle against doubts. 'Okay, Johannes.'

The lieutenant waits for the returning guards. He is kindly towards them, for they are scarcely out of their teens. He asks them their first names.

'Arbi, sir.'

'Teguh, sir.'

'Then take good care of the prisoner. Bring him a bowl of tonight's soup, Arbi.'

'But, sir – the captain specially –'

'Do as I say! If the prisoner requests water, give it to him.' Gani smiles in the dark. 'And one day Greenboots may acknowledge your kindness in his book.'

Teguh is amazed. 'This is Greenboots, sir?'

'Now do you understand why the prisoner must be well treated?'

Teguh and Arbi stare with new eyes at the broken man in the cage. Teguh's jaw has dropped open. He points at Greenboots. 'You're famous!'

Hans cannot bring himself to be amused. He turns his back, for these men have the blood of his friends on their hands.

Lieutenant Gani gestures the soldiers away from the prisoner's cage. 'We shall leave you in peace, Herr Mueller.'

Peace! Greenboots listens to the whispering forest. The fight has not gone out of him completely. 'There will never be peace, Lieutenant.'

'No?'

'Not until there is freedom.'

6

RESCUE IN THE STORM

Muyu and Lyana have watched the young lieutenant in his conversation with Greenboots, though from this distance in the forest they have heard nothing. They have, however, seen Gani slip a can of drink through the bars of the cage.

Lyana wonders, 'Could this be a friend?'

Muyu has one view only: the lieutenant is guilty of murdering the tribe; he and the others. Spots of heavy rain have begun to fall through the sky-black leaves: spears from the heavens, say the tribes when such a storm occurs. Long ago the thunder had released murmurs of warning yet only now has it provoked the rainstorm to break.

The two guards are back in position after the smoking-break granted them by Lieutenant Gani who has retired to his tent. Now comes the lightning, and the rain doubles its force.

Muyu wills the guards to go and seek shelter; and indeed this is what Arbi suggests to Teguh. 'Just till the storm is over?'

Teguh does not answer, afraid more of Captain Selim's temper than that of the storm. He squats down, makes his own protective cage of arms and legs, cradling his rifle on his knees.

Lyana wipes the rain from her hair; slowly shakes her head. 'We can rescue Hans only if we kill the guard.'

Muyu nods, understanding Lyana's words but not her meaning until she adds, 'And that would be wrong.'

At first Hans Mueller thinks his guards have reconsidered the risks of desertion and are returning to sentry duty. The lightning illuminates two figures approaching. Though one lens of his spectacles is shattered, though the jagged edges of glass send sparks into his eye, Greenboots instantly recognizes his friends.

'Muyu!'

The wooden bar to Greenboots' cage is slipped upwards and then used as a lever to lift the hatch. Two pairs of hands ease him on to his feet – unsteady feet, numb with cold – but all at once feet made for escaping.

Lyana takes his arm, presses her shoulder under him. He winces with pain. 'I think something's broken.' He is feeble yet his relief is a flood which carries him forward.

Lyana half smiles: Hans is covered in blood; his clothes are torn, jeans ripped at the seat – yet those Doc Martens are where they belong, itching to walk him into the forest and to safety the size of a raindrop.

Greenboots lives!

He glimpses her thoughts, whispers, 'The soldiers . . . wanted to toss up for my boots, but the lieutenant, he objected. And – wonders never cease! – Selim agreed with him . . . Without my Greenboots, who could prove I was me?'

They have reached the edge of the forest. The rain stops as abruptly as it began. The sky breaks open above them, showering the forest with stars.

Also broken open is the slumber of Lieutenant Johannes Gani. The storm ruffled his sleep but it is this eerie silence which shakes him awake. He leans up on his elbow, head spinning with the power of Selim's whisky.

It's time to meet the prisoner. Yet Gani now has second thoughts about what had seemed such a brilliant plan – to rescue Greenboots; take him deep in the forest; then obey orders.

Task completed, Colonel Fario.

Dead?

And buried without trace, sir.

No witnesses?

None.

Your father will be the proudest man in the empire.

Thank you, sir.

A hero: that is all Gani ever wanted to be. Known, admired, pointed out in the street. Yet here is the hero-to-be racked with doubt, with indecision. Things could so easily go wrong. What if Greenboots truly escaped? I would be accused by Selim. He already resents me. And Greenboots is Selim's prize. What did the captain call him? His golden goose.

No Greenboots, no glory for either of us. And for me, disgrace.

Gani recalls Selim's words: 'Greenboots is my ticket to the cushiest posting this side of paradise – Bali! Women in grass skirts ripe for the picking.'

Gani also recalls Colonel Fario's words: 'Fail in your task, Lieutenant, and we will disown you. You might as well step off the governor's terrace by the cliff and fall into the sea.'

'Thank you, sir. You may depend on me.'

Gani tries to wind up his courage; his resolve. He rehearses the sins of Greenboots: Hans Mueller has filled the heads of the forest folk with impossible dreams; he has talked to them of rights which will never be granted them; of protection from progress which has proved a wicked deceit.

He has led the forest people to destruction.

'You must silence him, Lieutenant, for the power of his words could bring down an empire.'

Gani sighs: true, for the power of Greenboots' words has already affected him. His book makes plenty of sense.

'Oh, and Gani?'

'Colonel?'

'Be sure not to let Herr Mueller – how shall we say? – engage you in conversation. He could soften your resolve. The moment he speaks is the moment to take your dagger and slit his throat. Understand?'

Slit his throat. That is how it must be done. Gani stirs, yet he has permitted thoughts to delay action for too long. From across the village clearing the sentries are raising the night with their shouts.

The sight of the empty cage has forced Arbi and Teguh to take counsel; consider the reaction of Captain Selim to the news that they abandoned their post, allowed his glorious future to be snatched away because of a poxy rainstorm.

'Attack!' yells Arbi. 'We was attacked!'

Teguh is quick in support. 'They come at us from all sides.'

Gani bursts from his tent, demanding explanation.

'The whole tribe, sir, they come for Greenboots.'

'Impossible!' That is Selim's verdict. He thrusts past Gani. With his pistol he strikes Teguh to the ground. 'You were asleep, you vermin.'

'It 'appened so fast, sir,' cries Arbi, appealing to Lieutenant Gani. 'Twenty of 'em, wi' guns.'

Selim snatches the soldier's rifle, beats him with it till both guards are in a terrified pile in the mud at his feet.

Gani is fearful that the sentries will be shot. He has a good brain and at last it is beginning to work in his favour. He says, 'What has happened here, sir, proves your point, I think.'

'My point?' Selim's brain is a dull one and still befuddled with drink.

'That the war will only be over when we exterminate every tribesman between Soul Mountain and the sea.'

'I said that?'

'Yes, sir. What's held back our success is too much mercy, too much compassion for these people. To win this war we need to shed more blood, not less.'

'Very true.' Selim rediscovers his passion. 'But Greenboots?'

'How fast can a sick man run, sir? In the dark, with his ribs broken and a high fever?'

'Well said! My own thoughts exactly.' The vision of Bali, of white, palm-fringed sands and girls in grass skirts reoccupies a corner of Selim's mind. 'I want that man alive, Gani, understand me? Alive. But the pigs who took him, I want them roasted till their flesh stinks as far as the capital.'

Marquez has arrived. He has listened with relief – even satisfaction – at the news of Greenboots' escape. 'That proves something else, Captain Selim.' He places a special emphasis on the title *Captain*, as if to say, You're not a colonel yet.

'Proves what else?' snaps Selim. Marquez' interruption somehow extinguishes the alluring prospects of Bali, reminding the captain of the cold silence of his forest prison.

'Yeah, it proves that that head you took don't belong to the lad Muyu. Cheeky young sod has made the army look silly, him tiptoeing behind your sentries an' running off with the big prize – your golden goose. I guess that'll not look too good in the newspapers.'

The darkness hides Marquez' grin of pleasure at Captain Selim's discomfort. 'And of course, you know what that means?'

Selim is too depressed, too cold and too empty

of resolve at this moment to order Marquez to shut his mouth. 'You will inform us, I am sure.'

'Well, with that lad at large, new chief of the tribe, and Greenboots' wisdom to call on, I reckon it's you who'd better be watching your back.

'Correct, er, *Captain*?'

7

THE PURSUIT BEGINS

Stiff, crooked, his back an explosion of shooting pains, Hans Mueller lets Muyu and Lyana drag him to the shelter of the forest. There, he forces a pause, shakes his head. 'No use. Go . . . They will come after us.'

Lyana says, 'They will not let the Bearded One live. Come!'

'If they find me with you – nor will you live.'

'It is still dark,' argues Muyu. 'And the soldiers fear the forest.'

At the camp Marquez is protesting. Selim has ordered his workers to join the search. 'Not a civilian job, Captain. My men are too valuable to waste on native spears.'

'You expect us to wait till daylight?'

Lieutenant Johannes Gani has sensed his opportunity. 'He's right, sir. Too many men trampling the forest in the blind dark could spell disaster.'

'Then what do you suggest, Mr College Boy?'

'Let me go alone, sir – or perhaps with these two guards. It's a punishment they deserve.'

'And if they hightail it?'

'I shoot them, sir.'

Relieved that his men will be removing the

forest, not getting lost in it, Marquez says, 'In Greenboots' condition, they'll head for Riverville, what the natives call the Sad Place. Mueller's got a friend there. The storekeeper, Old Ruiz, is his chess-mate.' Marquez grins. He considers it a pretty good joke for this time of the morning, and repeats it, 'Chess-mate – checkmate, get it?'

Selim has not been listening. 'You will pursue Mueller, Gani. By first light I will call up helicopter support. I shall pay a little visit to the Sad Place, and when I've finished with it, it'll be the No-Place.' He too can make a joke. 'Get it, Marquez?'

'Yes, very amusing, Captain.'

'And I want Hawks. Three of them from Britain were unpacked last week. We'll get them to stretch their wings.'

Marquez thinks this is also a joke. 'Hawk aircraft? To catch a sick cripple and a couple of kids?'

'The ravines, man – only the Hawks can prise out the Resistance in those parts.'

Marquez protests, 'You're supposed to be keeping the peace round here, Captain, not making war.'

Selim's day promises the action he loves. His gloom has lifted. He spares a moment for one final joke. 'With Gani on the ground, myself with thirty men sharpening our knives in Riverville and Hawks ready to machine-gun everything that moves between here and the ocean, I think this game of chess is definitely close to checkmate.'

Marquez sighs. 'You're forgetting something, Captain.'

'And what is that?'

'One of the pieces on the board is Mother Forest.'

Selim insists on having the last laugh. 'Then chop her down!'

With Hans' arms over their shoulders, his legs shaking with every stride, Muyu and Lyana have stumbled and slid down the great valley wall, its steepness sometimes levelling out to an almost comfortable angle, then pitching down again at a gradient which, with a false step, could send all three hurtling into space.

Mother Forest, muses Lyana, is unhappy. Perhaps this has been the wrong decision. And it is hers – Lyana's – to take Hans to hospital in the capital, with a first stop at the Sad Place. 'Then we can follow the river.'

Hans has said, 'Old Ruiz will sort me out . . . though I guess that's the first place they'll look for me.'

Muyu agreed: the Sad Place was the Bad Place. He had wanted to go to the high mountain for safety. But Hans had said, 'No, while I've strength to wag my tongue, I want to have my say, speak to the delegation. What happened to your people, Muyu, must be told to the world.'

The ground is drenched. The trees still shed the storm. The earth pulls them downwards. Thick ferns are all that they can hold on to. Even the trees seem dizzy with the drop below them.

'I won't make it.'

'We'll soon reach the river.'

'I've no strength. My skull, I think they . . .' He too tries a joke. 'Spilled out all my brains, what few I had.'

The heart is going out of Greenboots. He thinks he is dying. For certain, he is dozing, head slanting sideways and backwards into the soaked fern. There is a faint light above the forest. Dawn has arrived quicker than they expected.

'At least there are no soldiers.' Lyana's mind is on the journey before them, a challenge even for a fit man. Also, should they manage to follow the course of the river it would be days before they reached the capital.

Muyu has never been to the city, but he knows its distance. 'A boat,' he says. 'We must go by the river, not on land.'

Hans' eyes are closed. They had thought he was asleep, but he murmurs, 'My friend Ruiz has a boat. Outboard motor. Good thinking, Muyu.' His mind wanders. 'Emily likes going on boats. And she's great on surfboards. Me, I can't even hold on to one. Useless, really.'

The thought of Emily Bryson coming to cover the visit of the United Nations delegation for her newspaper revives Hans' spirits.

She's on her way! She'll have that bottle of whisky. Tobacco. A change of underpants. 'I need to smarten up. Have a shave. Splash some of that Brut stuff over me.'

He makes his companions smile: he is almost the Greenboots they have learned to love. He is calling out, 'Can you hear me, Emily? Scotch whisky only. No substitutes. Twenty-one years in the cask. And get *The Times* on the phone, and the *Washington Post*.'

He almost falls headlong into the valley. His route would have been halted by a rock escarpment now beginning to glitter in the dawn light; then it would have descended into the gloom of a ravine even the army's best helicopters or its Hawk fighters fear to penetrate.

Instead Muyu and Lyana catch Hans' arms. It is Muyu's turn to joke: 'Remember, Greenboots, it is Lyana who is the angel. So please let her do the flying!'

They cross below overhanging crags. Sweeping contours of brown shale are sprayed by cascades from above; and the sound of this part of the forest is of waters roaring, from the high mountain, from caverns and from waterfalls plunging into mists of fine spray.

Rock faces open into sparkling grottoes, like jewelled temples built only for those brave enough to scale such heights, mad enough to ignore the vertical fall and the fierce attack of diving streams. They rest. Beside Muyu there are figures inscribed in the rock in red and black dye; hunters of the past; evidence of the ancient lineage of his people.

'These pictures on the rock – wonderful. As old as the pyramids, I reckon. See – your history, Muyu. It's a sign from Mother Forest that we're going to survive. Pity Selim smashed my camera.'

Suddenly the recollection of another missing

treasure pitches Greenboots into despondency. 'My notebook!' It is as though he has discovered the loss of his soul. 'Everything – gone!'

Lyana takes hold of Greenboots' hand and gently leads it over her shoulder. He recognizes his rucksack. 'Safe?'

'Safe – all your words, all your thoughts.'

'What did I say, Muyu? She is truly an angel in disguise. Angel of the Forest. Look after these things for me, Lyana, for the present. And if we come out of all this, I will put your name and Muyu's in the dedication.'

He shrugs. 'Doesn't sound much, I know. Not worth a cold hamburger, really. But where I come from it's . . .' He gazes at the companions who have saved his life and upon whom his life now depends. 'It's a token of deep gratitude and most of all – friendship.'

Hans pauses, eyes scouring the forest: everything that has happened is churning in his head – the attack, the deaths, the beatings; the destruction of a tribe, of a way of life reaching back beyond the horizons of time. 'It is so difficult . . . to cling on to hope.'

He is beginning to fade once more. He stares at his companions. They are his hope; and yet by allowing them to rescue him, letting them plan this perilous journey to the capital instead of retreating to the high mountain, he is probably signing their death warrant.

He will not give voice to his worst fear, that he, because of his wagging tongue, because of his boastful writings, has brought on the death of Muyu Father's tribe.

Perhaps, he wonders, I am no better than those white men who landed on the shores of the New World and spread mortal diseases among the native peoples.

In my case, the mortal disease has been words of liberty.

Lyana has wiped his wounds, given him life-restoring water. Now she stands, remains for a moment perfectly still, head turned to hear the smallest sound of the forest. Muyu too is up and listening.

'Soldiers!'

8

TREASON

They are descending once more. Great ribs of light stand broad as trees and in their higher reaches there are rainbows. Hans pauses, points in delight:

'Rainbows for good luck!'

Gingerly Muyu and Lyana lift him down rocks so steep they block out any view of the ground below, yet not so steep that they exclude the dazzling sky. Soon the contours of the ground grow more friendly. Lyana takes Hans' weight.

He senses her trembling and guesses at her growing fear. 'You do not need to come into the village, Lyana, if you feel . . .'

'I shall come.'

For Lyana the Sad Place had been more than sad; there, for a period, with her family gone, she had been captive in the tin huts. She once told Hans what happened there. At the time, Hans had listened and, thinking he was speaking wisdom, said, 'You must bury the painful memories in forgetfulness. Unless you do, they will rise up to torment you like the ghosts of the forest. And for ever.'

'I will never forget.' And now she fears the prospect of returning, of passing the tin huts at the edge of the village, of seeing the tall fences topped with razor wire; of recognizing the compound where she and her friend Maria attempted their escape.

She shudders at the bitter force of memory. They reach flat ground. Lyana is back in the nightmare, for they have strayed into a clearing full of crosses; crosses like that which she made for Maria.

Some of the graves bear scribbled inscriptions; others have been left without record; for hadn't the next wave of troops been just behind, sweeping woman and child before it, turning the island into a forest of blood?

Only now does Muyu feel the full woe of the death of Muyu Father, and the loss which will be all the worse for a death without ceremony. 'What did they do with Muyu Father's body?' he asks Hans.

They pause, rest in a clearing blind with sunlight. The last mist has cleared. Greenboots lies to be kind: 'I remember nothing.'

'One day,' Muyu responds, 'I shall return.'

'Of course you will. Me too!'

'I shall meet Muyu Father once more. I shall take him and bury him on Soul Mountain.'

Hans Mueller nods. 'To be sure, his spirit has flown there already.'

Muyu is not comforted. 'Only when the family of Muyu Father places him in the ground will he know rest.'

Lyana chooses the words which soften Muyu's

grief. 'However far we travel, Muyu, however far the soldiers drive us from our homeland – we shall return.'

They stand together; she hugs him. That way she conceals her tears, shed not only for Muyu Father and so many of the tribe, but for Maria; for her own family, whose only sin was being able to read.

Her grief is for all those of her people who fled from the Bapak armies, from the merciless Green Berets and the British Hawks whose bombs and gunfire slaughtered the villagers even on the sacred heights of Soul Mountain.

'One day,' says Muyu.

'Yes – one day!'

At the edge of the escarpment half a mile above, Lieutenant Johannes Gani focuses his binoculars. 'That's Greenboots all right. And two others. A girl and a youth – limping: the boy chief.'

He talks as though he is alone. 'So Captain Selim wants them roasted alive. As they say, first catch your pig. Well, she's an eyeful all right. And the one person in the tribe who can read. Thanks to Mueller, she's fluent in German and English, I believe. Still, it's a mystery how somebody with brains can put up with such a life.'

'The capt'n sez the tribes ain't got no brains, sir,' comments Arbi.

Teguh contradicts, 'No, he sez the tribes 'as got one brain between 'em, but it got lost down an 'ole centuries ago.'

'Oh?' Gani lowers his binoculars. 'And the rest of us are so clever, are we?' He has six soldiers with him – Arbi, Teguh and four islanders. As surety for the survival of their loved ones, in jail in the capital, these 'volunteers' serve the enemy.

Gani expects them to desert at any moment. He even hopes they will. He fears that otherwise their guns, with only the forest as witness, might be turned on him.

Teguh is agreeing with his lieutenant. 'What use 're brains i' these woods? Two and two don't mean nothin'. What y'need's a good nose, a pair o' sharp ears an' plenty o' puff. These folks run rings round the military, always will.'

Gani remembers he is an officer with a mission. 'Not today, gentlemen.'

Arbi says, 'I tells y' who I'm sorry for – them villagers down there. 'Cause the captain's i' one of 'is moods.'

'Meaning?' asks Gani.

'Meanin' they'd better scarper or say their prayers.'

'Specially the women,' adds Teguh. 'Beggin' yer pardon, sir, but it's disgust'n' what 'e gets up to.'

The exchange of opinions is interrupted by the distant purr of a helicopter, which fast becomes a clattering roar above them.

'There 'e goes, sir, the Butcher wi' the Shades.'

'I seem to recall,' says Gani, 'that Riverville is under our protection.'

69

The two soldiers glance at each other: this officer is wet behind the ears.

Arbi explains: 'First off, the captain'll drink Old Ruiz' bar dry. Then the fireworks'll start explodin'. Not a soul'll be safe, not even you, sir.'

Lyana, Muyu and Hans Mueller also watch the helicopter as it passes overhead. Greenboots says, 'I'm surprised they've not sent in the Hawks to ferret us out. Nice folks, the British. They call themselves a freedom-loving people. Yet they sell arms to every dictatorship in the world.'

'Same with the Yanks. Ninety per cent of the weapons the Bapaks used to invade this island came from the Land of the Free.'

Greenboots' speech ends abruptly as rough ground causes him to lose balance. He trips, tumbles helplessly, cracks his skull against a dead tree. His head-wound opens. Gently, Lyana and Muyu lay Greenboots on his back.

'Sorry, folks. Talking and walking – too much for me, I'm afraid.'

Lyana teases out the wood splinters from the gash in his forehead, bathes the wound. Despite the heat, Greenboots is shaking. He is barely conscious. 'The fever is worse,' she says. 'You must have rest.'

Muyu watches the forest slope. Somewhere above them there is the brush of boots striding through grass and scrub. His instincts tell him that he must draw the pursuers off, yet to leave Lyana alone with Greenboots would mean that they might never reach the village or the river.

Lyana decides, 'We must let them pass.' Muyu joins her in tearing down branches heavy with leaves. They make a nest of green.

Gani and the soldiers are following the stream. They are less than twenty minutes behind their quarry now. They have just paused at yet another cemetery in the forest. Gani is strangely moved: all these people – children too – probably on the run, at risk of slaughter, yet finding time to bury their dead.

His companions too voice their feelings. Arbi comments, 'These could be our folks, Teguh.'

'Not right!' asserts Teguh.

Gani attempts to speak up for his government in this matter. 'They had a choice.'

Arbi rounds on the young officer. 'What choice is that, sir? To 'ave the military runnin' riot through their 'omes, torturin' their men, takin' their women – is that what y'call choice? And when they 'ide i' the forest, to 'ave them Hawks an' Broncos machine-gunnin' 'em?'

'I mean, like,' comes in Arbi, 'it's not as if the Distant Masters let the people go on growin' their crops.'

'True,' says Teguh with a sad shake of the head. 'The gover'ment sends in planes wi' chemicals as destroy every damn thing, animals too.'

Arbi: 'It's 'orrible.'

''Orrific more like,' asserts Teguh. 'Y'should try

71

goin' in an' clearin' up after one o' these raids, Lieutenant.'

Gani knows these men are talking treason, but he does not stop them. Treason has begun to interest him.

Teguh: 'What's more, them chemicals don't just ruin the crops, sir, they poison folk. First it's shittin', then it's the vomitin'. Eats away their insides. All they can do's stagger off into the forest an' die. Bloody diabolical, sir, if y'ask me.'

Late in the day for a trained spy, Lieutenant Johannes Gani has become suspicious of his two gallant sentries. First, Arbi spoke not of the government in Jakarta, but of the Distant Masters, a term used only by the tribespeople. Second, unlike the other soldiers Gani has met, Arbi and Teguh do not refer to the forest as the jungle. Rather, they speak of it with a suppressed love.

Am I among traitors?

Gani's body seems to have anticipated the answer to his question. The sweat from his hair still drains into his eyes yet he feels the chill of fear. Until now he has scarcely looked his subordinates in the face. Now, when he does so in dawning terror, he stares down the barrels of the soldiers' guns. 'What's happening?'

Arbi has advanced. 'We're advisin' you – sir – not to go to the Sad Place.' Gani is thrust to the ground, his rifle torn from his shoulder, his pistol from the holster at his belt.

Teguh says, 'Sorry 'bout this, Lieutenant. We

thinks y'might be a decent sort, but yer 'ead's too full o' rules and reg'lations.'

Gani is allowed back on to his feet. They're going to shoot me. 'You are Resistance?'

He receives no reply. Teguh turns to the volunteer soldiers. 'Okay, you lot, take yer chance – scram!'

The islanders need no second invitation. They melt into the forest and the forest holds its breath as they pass.

Gani is told to put his hands above his head. It is all done with an air of apology. He says, 'You know what this means? To disarm an officer of the empire is high treason.'

'Only if yo' talk, sir.'

'Then you're going to kill me?'

Arbi considers the question, then turns to Teguh, nods. 'Tie 'im!'

Gani is astonished. 'You brought rope?' The whole thing has been planned from the start. 'So you intend leaving me here to rot?'

Teguh tries to be reassuring. 'If you done yer survival trainin', sir, you'll be out o' this lot quicker'n two scorpions 'avin' sex!'

'What will I tell the captain?'

Arbi is stern, impatient to be off. 'That you shot us two fer desertin'. Left us like two 'eaps o' compost i' the forest. That was yer idea, wa'n't it?'

Gani is silent.

Teguh binds Gani's legs. 'We reckon you mean no good to old Greenboots, Lieutenant. A case of

– oops, 'is throat's cut, eh? Dead men speak no lies.'

Arbi has a final piece of advice. 'Y'd best watch your ass, Joey, mate, cos it's only a matter o' time before the captain susses you out.' He laughs. 'Then we'll not be the only ones guilty o' treason!'

The Sound of Gunfire

Essentially a man of peace, Marquez was to have no idea how his parting words to Captain Selim were to lead to an act of war – the destruction of yet another island village. Marquez disliked Selim as much as he hated the heat of the forest, yet his words delayed the flight of the Alouette:

'I'd look into that young officer of yours, Captain. Everything about him is fishy.'

Selim had also felt uneasy about Lieutenant Gani. 'What are you getting at, Marquez?'

'How come he knows so much about Green-boots?'

'Because he's read the man's poxy book.'

'Okay, but why insist on taking those two with him, the guards whose negligence brought about this situation in the first place?'

'He took eight men.'

'Six of them were islanders, jerks who'll take themselves off quicker than leaves in a thunderstorm.'

Marquez' hunch about Lieutenant Gani was correct in every detail – except one. 'In my view, Captain, you've a viper in your midst. Gani is Resistance. And his plan's as clear as daylight – to rescue Greenboots from your clutches.'

'Nonsense!'

'Think about it, Captain. Your golden goose is about to be snatched from under your nose.'

'There's no evidence –'

'No? Then how come Gani never fired a shot yesterday when you sorted out the tribe?'

'How can you know that?'

'I have eyes. And who was it permitted your guards to take a smoke last night, allowing a couple of kids to rescue Captain Selim's passport to Bali?'

Marquez walked away, casting his final, crushing words towards the high forest. 'Huh, officers who get taken for a ride by their juniors, Captain, don't ever make colonel.'

The Alouette, with a dozen soldiers on board, is hovering over the Sad Place which is strung untidily along the near bank of the river. Even at this height, Selim feels the cloying heat. There is no escape from it as there seems to be no escape from the Resistance.

Could even Marquez be a member? After all, he'd been bitterly critical of the shooting.

Selim issues orders: the village is to be searched, every house, every shack, starting with the stores and bar of Old Ruiz. 'I want all the males you find assembled by the compound fence. And that includes Lieutenant Gani.'

The treetops sway as the Alouette circles the

village and descends towards cleared ground beside the barbed wire encampment stretching up the hillside from the river.

This is where Selim had been commandant on his first posting. As a result of certain events – the accusation of rape and the unexplained death of a native girl – Selim had been relieved of his post. He had been lieutenant then: his promotion to captain was conditional upon his operating away from civilian areas; in the forest where only the trees and the insects were witness to his butchery.

Yet Selim cannot entirely drive away a chill of horror at memories prompted by the sight of the camp: he remembers the face of the girl, her last living expression of agony.

Her name, he recalls, was Maria: in fact, it had been her friend he had wanted. The beautiful and mysterious one. Yet she had escaped. Or caught a bullet and died in the forest. Her name was Anna; or could it have been Lyana?

Selim scours the faces of his men. 'Thirsty, gentlemen?'

'You bet, sir!'

'Okay. Then it's drinkies first and duty later.'

The forest has drawn down the heat of the afternoon, sucked it in between shade and open space, trapped it; and heat has added to heat. It is the hour of slumber. The breeze rests. The clouds in the sky hang unmoving. Nothing stirs except the slow slide of sweat.

Lyana's thoughts are not very distant from

those of Captain Selim. For her, the Sad Place means barbed wire, beatings; her own humiliation and most of all the murder of her friend.

The memory is still there, in every detail: the attempted escape; the hole in the fence, the alarm, the bullets in the night; and Maria impaled on the razor wire; to be dragged off with the razors still in her flesh.

One day the story of it will be told in Hans' book. The story is in his log which she carries in the rucksack over her shoulder. Muyu had asked, 'Why did you let Hans write it all down about Maria? That is bad luck.'

'Not if what happened to my friend is remembered.'

'We remember.'

'I want people always to remember.'

Muyu had not understood; in a way, neither did Lyana. It was not the forest way to hold on to time; as it were, to save it, turn it into a statue or a shrine. Muyu had taken her hands, cupped them, touched her palms with his finger. 'That is where Maria is.'

And now Muyu Father, Dani – all the men of the tribe – were gone from the arms of Mother Forest. Instinctively Lyana folds one hand over the other as if to protect the spirits of the departed.

Higher in the forest, sweat has come to the rescue of Lieutenant Johannes Gani. It has slid through the ropes that bind his hands, soaking them, slackening them. His head, dizzy with the heat, is also filled with times past. This right hand once shook that of the president himself.

How smart Johannes' uniform had been; how proud he felt as he paraded in front of the presidential palace, with his father, the general, looking on with deepest satisfaction.

The ball which followed the passing-out parade could have taken place in Paris or St Petersburg in another age; and on Johannes' arm, making him the envy of the regiment, was Regina – perfection itself – daughter of the American ambassador.

In those moments he felt only destiny could rob him of a glorious and happy future. Even now his fingers recall the silken splendour of Regina's ballgown, the slimness of her waist; even now the scent of her perfume is in his nostrils.

His hands are free. He lies back for a few moments, exhausted with the effort. I stink. How're things in Jakarta, Regina? Got a new boyfriend? Or am I still in with a chance; still on trial?

It had been something of a joke: 'A soldier isn't a soldier in my view,' Regina had said, laughing, relishing the moonlight in her hair, 'unless he's seen some action. My last boyfriend fought in the Gulf War.'

Come back with medals – who said that, Regina or Johannes' father? How mad; how stupid all that seems now. He has almost worked his ankle ropes free. I should have told her to come and join me if she's so impressed with heroes.

Bloody heroes!

Stiffly he stretches, slowly stands, reaches out

to a tree to keep his balance. Somehow he has
gone off Regina. I think I've shit in my pants. How
about that, Reggie? It's probably no less than your
last boyfriend did in the Gulf, shit in his pants.

And this thought brings Gani sweatily, stink-
ingly, back to the present: what to do next? He
reaches for the water bottle. As he does so, he
hears gunfire from the village.

10

ENCOUNTER WITH THE PAST

The shooting stops. Slowly over the Sad Place a cloud of smoke climbs above the level of the trees. It hangs, thickens; and in the breezeless dusk lazily spreads towards the river.

Muyu, Lyana and Hans Mueller have waited. They had been about to enter the village when the helicopter appeared, hovered for a while like an eagle glaring down at its prey, then swooped to earth.

They have taken cover; trembled at the scene in the village where sounds without vision stoke the imagination: first shouts, sick with panic, stopped by a single gunshot; a pause, then the cold staccato of automatic rifle fire. Tracks and paths are suddenly filled with villagers dashing for the protection of Mother Forest.

Lyana asks Hans, 'Where is this boat of Old Ruiz'?'

Greenboots has scarcely strength to draw breath. 'At the rear of the bar ... there's a ... slope to the river. A wooden jetty.' He tries to smile. 'Lovely view on a good day.'

'He will lend us his boat?'

'He's my chess partner – of course he will. No questions asked.'

'And he will give us supplies.' Lyana makes to move.

'No. That's not on . . . not now. Too dangerous, Lyana.'

'You need medicine, food.'

'I'll eat roots.' He is shaking his head. 'Selim is on the rampage. Just check on the boat, that's all I ask.'

Lyana is worried for Muyu. His own wound needs treatment. He is dragging his leg and is in agony. 'Let me go alone,' she suggests.

Muyu will not hear of it. He has a picture in his head of the village, of riflemen going from house to house, leaving each an inferno. 'No – you will stay, Lyana. Look after Hans.'

'We go together.'

'That's best,' decides Greenboots. He does not mind being left in the forest. He prefers it. If I'm dying, he thinks, they'll be better off without me.

He plays calm and collected, takes out his pipe. 'Well, comrades, the sooner you go, the sooner you'll be back.'

Lyana makes Hans promise he will stay exactly where they leave him. 'Please – do not wander.'

'Is it okay for my mind to wander?'

At a glimpse of soldiers ahead, Lyana pulls Muyu off the track. The mud stirred up by last night's storm now steams in the last heat of the day. A dozen troops have turned the Sad Place into a ruin, consumed by fire. The forest is black with smoke.

Strutting down the side of the track, comically out of place yet seemingly indifferent to the destruction all around it, is a cockerel. It is proudly accompanied by four hens. A few feet away, a single body lies in a ditch. Further on, where the barbed-wire compound forms a corner between the centre of the village and the forest beyond, women and children are lined up. They face the wall of an outbuilding, guarded by one soldier.

Where the track branches towards the river there is the sound of a transistor radio playing a love ballad sung by Elvis Presley. Three soldiers squat round it as if warming themselves at a camp fire.

'Drunk,' whispers Lyana.

The painted sign of Old Ruiz' Universal Stores and Bar-Restaurant is bold and unmistakable; and, despite the fires that have destroyed the rest of the village, seemingly unharmed.

There is a front veranda, real glass in the windows – though some of it is in need of repair. Behind the wooden store is a fenced area where ducks are gathered for a feed they will never receive.

Several wooden tables and chairs stand deject-edly on a lawn decorated with tubs of flowers. The view from such tables, claims the notice over Ruiz' door, is the second-best vista on the island (the other being across the ocean from the gov-ernor's residency).

Ruiz has been known for his loyalty – that is, Hans had explained, loyalty to everyone who demanded it: the government in Jakarta ('God bless the president!'), the troops of the occupying army ('You all deserve medals!') and to the Resistance ('Silence is my second name, comrades!').

Most genuinely, however, Ruiz' affections have been for the people of the forest. He has lived among them for twenty years. If their friend was Hans Mueller, then, Ruiz swore, 'Hans Mueller is my friend!'

At this moment Captain Selim is no friend of Old Ruiz. Though the card in the window says BAR CLOSED TILL FURTHER NOTICE, Selim makes and breaks the rules around here. In a brown glow reflected off jugs of polished brass hanging from the bar counter, Selim holds a gin bottle in one hand and in the other his Kalashnikov rifle.

Ruiz sits in front of him, below him, bound hand and foot to an oak rocking chair. In slurred words, Selim has been saying, 'I had a dream, Ruiz. Two old friends met by candlelight. Your good self and the man who is going to make my fortune, your old comrade Greenboots.' Selim's gaze rests on the table beside Ruiz, the surface of which is marked out for chess.

'It's a war game, isn't it, chess? Funny, I ought to be good at it.' Selim has crossed to the bar counter. He brings a box of chess pieces to the table, slides open the lid and empties the box. 'Now how are they laid out? Foot soldiers at the front, correct? The pawns in the game.

'Like me and my men. Sent out into this shithole

to be destroyed by nigs with spears and bows and arrows, poisoned by snakes, shat on by monkeys and stung by mosquitoes.

'And behind them, folks of privilege, eh? Our bosses, who swan about while we do their dirty work. Understand, Ruiz, the nature of the game? I think you do.'

Selim holds up a bishop and a knight. 'See these. You'll guess which bishop: the pesky priest of this island, with a bigger mouth even than Greenboots. I intend to take him out personally one day. And this? Recognize this, Ruiz?'

Tightly gagged, the old man can only shake his head. He is having difficulty breathing. His face is swollen and his eyes protrude unnaturally.

'No? Look closer. A knight. Yes, a knight in shining armour. Only he's got himself knocked about a bit lately. Your friend, Ruiz, the white knight; and he's heading in this direction. That's what my dream told me.'

Selim now holds up a castle. 'The knight rides to the castle. He'll expect some help, I guess. And that is where I want you to assist the war effort like one of these little pawns.

'Believe me, Ruiz, the only reason why this dump is not already a heap of ashes is because I want Greenboots to come limping in for his very last game of chess.'

Ruiz glares at his captor. He is struggling to breathe.

'Not happy? Well, never mind. I could very well be making the wrong move myself in ordering my men out of the village. My preference, you see, is for poker. There's more risk involved.

'But I was telling you about this wonderful dream of mine. In comes Greenboots, sees these chess pieces all over the place. Good grief! And his old pal Ruiz bound and gagged. What a good thing Selim has moved off into the forest to gather a few more scalps. Read me?'

Selim drinks. The bottle is almost empty. 'I think you do. But what you will fail to grasp is the connection between your friend and my future, between the hero of the downtrodden and the dancing girls of Bali.'

The captain points to his Ray-bans. 'See these, Ruiz? They're the only goddam thing that makes me special. Except my temper. But things are going to change. Come this time next month I'll be having myself measured for an Armani suit and . . . Ah, but I see I bore you.

'None of your damned business anyway. You will excuse me, then, while I make myself comfortable in the old back room. Don't worry yourself – I'll leave the door open, just in case you need anything.

'Okay, Ruiz? Good. Now let's see if my dream is about to come true.'

One of the soldiers listening to the transistor has glanced at his watch. He switches off the music. The soldiers get to their feet. They are joined by others. Without a word, as if at a hidden signal, they head for the forest.

As far as Lyana and Muyu can guess, the village is deserted. Even the women and children of the compound seem to have vanished in the approaching dusk.

Lyana says: 'Greenboots needs things –'

'Not the store.'

'They've gone!'

'It could be a trap.'

'Hans will die on us unless we can get proper food. And your leg, it needs cleaning, bandaging. Disinfectant.'

Muyu says, 'I will survive.' Yet he does not believe himself. 'Perhaps –'

'Not perhaps. We must risk it.'

Muyu agrees. 'Together.'

She is stubborn. 'The boat is the most important thing, Muyu. I will go to the store. I will be careful.'

He shakes his head. 'I am not going to leave you.'

'Listen, if there is no boat, then we must take Hans back into the forest. If we have to do that, it's all the more important we get what we need.'

He is unhappy. 'I do not like this place.'

'Then let us do what we have to do and get out.' She repeats, 'I will be careful.'

Muyu knows her: no argument will sway Lyana once she has set her path. He hands her his dagger. She knows he will not leave her unless she agrees to take it.

He smiles. 'Maybe you will bring us a duck, eh?' She watches him move, ever-limping, along the wire fence housing the hungry ducks. They rush over towards him, raising a storm of complaints.

Duck roasted on a spit over a fire in the safety of Mother Forest, with the tribe gathered together once more – what a dream that would be.

She wonders, did Muyu hear her when she called, 'Go back to Hans, I will meet you there.'

Lyana feels a single drop of rain. This storm will put out the fires. Then the villagers will return, start their lives all over again. Until the next time.

What was it I must get for Greenboots? Beer, tobacco, bread, aspirin, a bottle of disinfectant. More bandages for Muyu. Oh, and some clothes. If we're to talk to the United Nations, we need to smarten up. Ask Old Ruiz to put it on my account.

Lyana waits till the ducks return to picking the ground for their supper. There is a veranda at the back of the store as well as the front. She pauses before reaching the first window. She hears rain beginning to drum on the sloping roof above her. The veranda has been repaired with corrugated sheeting which amplifies the sound of the storm.

She peers into the dark interior of the bar. It is empty – or so it seems at first glance. She passes the window, glancing inside again as she does so. She halts, recognizing a figure of an old man in the chair, his back to the window.

Could Old Ruiz have slept through the attack on the village?

The door is unlatched and slightly ajar. She can

almost slip through without pushing the door; but not quite. In easing her way through, Lyana gives the door a nudge and its treacherous hinges squeak loud enough to disturb anyone not in a deep sleep.

The head of Old Ruiz is tilted forward. It does not move as she approaches across the rush-strewn earthen floor. She sees a table beside the old man, the surface covered with chess pieces.

He has been waiting for Hans.

Now Lyana sees the ropes which bind Ruiz to his rocking chair; and the gag which has forced his mouth wide open. She stands in front of Ruiz, waits. She is surprised that even the storm has not disturbed him for it beats fiercely on the store roof.

'Señor Ruiz?' She circles the old man, reaches out to touch – to wake – the slumbering store keeper; and in the same instant, draws back.

Ruiz is dead.

Lyana retreats, yet is compelled to return, to examine Hans' friend. There are no wounds that she can see. For several moments she stares at the old man. The ropes and the gag are cruelly tight: perhaps they have proved too much for one whose blood moved slowly.

Perhaps fear pounded too hard for an ailing heart.

For a while she cannot decide what to do next. The storm and this scene before her, of such a sad parting with life, slow her own blood, empty her limbs of the power to serve.

Because her back is turned to the bar, and to the store room behind it, and because the storm would disguise the sound of even a heavy footfall, Lyana is unaware of the figure emerging from darkness behind her.

Though this female apparition, beautiful as a postcard, had not featured in Captains' Selim's wonderful dream, he isn't going to complain. In fact, the captain muses, this need not be my unlucky day after all.

She is gorgeous.

Yet, strangely for him, Selim also hesitates to act, to disturb the stillness. Old Ruiz' death is an inconvenience, not something planned. And after all, Ruiz had his own fame – he could mix the best cocktail on the island.

There is something else which checks Selim's will to act: this girl, the shape of her, the poise of her neck and head – does she not remind him of someone; though not her age or height? He racks his brains. Nothing connects.

Selim decides he has dwelt long enough in the realm of thought. He raises and points his Kalashnikov. 'I do not think I have had the pleasure of your acquaintance, miss.'

Lyana spins round. She gasps with shock – and then recognition. Her hands rise up involuntarily as if to protect her breasts. She fits the face to one she knew long ago and had fought to forget: that expression, those eyes, that arrogant look of cruelty.

Their exclamations collide in mid-air: 'You!'

To Lyana's lips now springs, not the name of Selim, the officer who had turned her life into a nightmare, but of his victim, and her friend:

Maria!

11

THE SCREAM

Muyu has reached Old Ruiz' jetty. It was once a stopping-off place for trading craft, a busy point of exchange where crops of rice, maize, sweet potato and cassava were shipped to the capital and where supplies for the village were docked and stored in the warehouse adjoining Ruiz' store.

With the war, trade virtually ceased as both villagers and forest folk, in terror of the army, either drifted to the city or escaped to the mountains.

Ruiz' own boat – a rower with outboard motor – is riding the swollen river, being swept by it from side to side, wrenching at its mooring. The jetty is unsafe. Planks are damaged, spars missing. Where they have not snapped off altogether, uprights are bent or split.

Muyu knows what this storm will do to the river. I must bring Greenboots. He glances momentarily towards Old Ruiz' store. No sign of Lyana yet. He is not worried. The place is quiet and the soldiers have gone into the forest.

He makes his way towards where they left Greenboots. The storm blinds and deafens him. We will not need the motor. The river will carry us to the ocean as fast as a bird flies.

Muyu reaches Hans Mueller who has not moved a limb save to protect his pipe from the rain.

'The boat – okay?' Greenboots asks. Muyu nods, helps him to his feet. 'And Lyana – don't say you let her go to the village?'

'She will meet us at the jetty. This way, Hans.'

The bank is steep and slippery. The forest howls with the storm – yet not so loudly as to drown the sudden scream that pierces the dusk.

A scream so chilling it seems to freeze the rain as it falls.

They both halt, turn. 'Lyana?' They wait, paralysed with shock. And the scream comes again.

Like the forest, Greenboots howls into the storm. 'It's her! You must go, Muyu.'

They are at the river. The storm now unleashes its full power. Strong winds join rain. The forest, as one tree, bends against the onslaught. It is like the end of the world.

The scream nevertheless goes on competing with the storm. It is horrible, and in the forest, the retreating soldiers sense it; pause; listen.

Lieutenant Johannes Gani also listens. He has had to avoid the track leading into the village for it is now a river of mud. He had been lost yet the smoke from the fires has proved a reliable compass.

He hears the screaming. It is coming from the store up the road. He thinks immediately of Selim, the Butcher in Shades. Has he turned the store into a torture chamber? It's all in Greenboots' book: haunting. Did we do that? And that? There is the picture of the room where the dead are stacked in their blood, the wall splashed with blood, the wall riddled with bullet holes.

The screaming persists for a moment competing with the storm; then falls silent. Gani hesitates: it could be me next. Yet he reminds himself, I am an officer of the second largest empire in the world. I must show resolution.

Muyu has left Greenboots beneath the jetty. He fears that the rain, turning the land into a flood, might sweep his friend into the river.

Hans waves him away. 'Don't worry about me – just find her!'

Muyu's leg, stiff with the cold, collapses under him, sending him spinning on to his face in mud. He grabs at wind-flattened reeds. The forest seems to be melting in the rain, the trees becoming streams, their leaves cascading like waterfalls.

Hans too feels the ground beneath him sliding. The river bank is breaking into chunks of soaked mud, slithering over its own edge. He reaches for the sturdiest pillar of the jetty. All that matters is to hold on to the rucksack.

He is dizzy. The rain is spattering in through the frail shelter of the jetty floor. 'Oh God, let nothing've happened to her!'

*

Gani has reached the veranda of Old Ruiz' place. He hesitates. He hears banging inside, like furniture being tipped over. He hears the crash of glass.

The ducks behind Ruiz' place seem as unhappy with the storm as humans. They are mute witnesses to the approach of Muyu, limping. He lunges at the enclosure, helps himself along, feet sliding at every step; then he stops, wrenches at a corner post.

Nothing works for him. The post snaps and all he's left with for a weapon is a rotted baton half a metre long. He hurls it away in disgust. He approaches the rear veranda. As he does so, the door swings open.

'Lyana!'

She is soaked in blood. It is over her face, her T-shirt, so darkly it obliterates the emblem of the whale. She carries Muyu's dagger in her hand. She walks down towards him as if in a trance, takes his hand, turns him round.

'What happened?'

'Hans – is he safe?'

'Yes, but –'

Lyana draws Muyu away, down the slope. It is slippery but she does not slip. The dagger seems to be fixed to her hand by invisible wires. She looks at it as she descends. A trickle of blood runs off the blade into the rain. She does not speak.

Gani has found the door of Ruiz' place ajar. He hesitates before entering; and eventually has no need to take another step. Out of the darkness

95

emerges a bent form, not screaming now, but groaning; whimpering like a beaten dog.

Captain Selim is stumbling from side to side, retching with the pain. His trouser belt must have come undone for his khaki denims are around his knees; and around everything – his bare legs, his knees, his ankles, his boots – is blood.

'Gani! Thank God!' He falls, holding himself, and where he holds himself his hands drip with blood. 'Get her – the girl – the girl!'

'Crazy!' Hans has opened his heavy eyes to see the rage of the river. His mind is drifting on its surface and he speaks to his young friend as if Muyu were beside him. 'We need to think again, Muyu. I'm a bad sailor. Can't swim.'

Greenboots peers through the sweeping curtain of rain. His sigh of relief challenges the voices of the forest. 'Lyana!'

He sees the blood, opens his mouth – but she passes him, checking her pace for an instant to leave against his cheek the gentlest touch of her hand.

'Lyana? The blood . . .'

With Muyu she is heaving the boat shorewards.

In her left hand Lyana carries a plastic carrier bag stuffed with provisions. 'Hold this, please.'

'But Ruiz – what's happened to him?'

Intent on sparing Greenboots further grief, Lyana ignores the question. Yet he persists. 'Grief, child – all that blood!'

Lyana joins Muyu in the river. They are up to

96

their waists. The jetty is rocking. The boat is rolling, shipping waves. The painter is tight to snapping point, spinning with river spray.

'Into the boat, Hans!'

Between them, Lyana and Muyu hold the craft steady. They ease their friend on board.

'I can't swim a stroke!'

Lyana remembers what Muyu has forgotten: 'The rucksack!' He returns to the bank, retrieves Greenboots' precious cargo.

Hans blinks in the rain. Terrible things have happened. He does not want to go on. 'Listen, you two – why don't you leave me?'

He receives no response and knows he does not deserve one. He draws in breath, haunted by the sight of her – a woman covered in blood.

Yes, so like the photos in his book.

He presumes she is bleeding. He finds strength to assist her aboard. He senses her blood between his fingers. 'Christ – where're you hurt, Lyana?'

She spares him two words: 'Not me!'

Hans sits back. Shock mixes with relief; with wonderment. He watches her. She reaches into the bulging shopping bag. She removes a hand-gun, a Browning. 'The captain will not be needing this for the present.' She hands it to him. 'In a moment the soldiers will come.'

Haggard with cold, convinced disaster has turned to catastrophe, Hans meekly takes the gun. He gazes at Lyana and for once in his life words desert him.

Lyana's thoughts dwell on her long-dead friend Maria: 'May Soul Mountain welcome you home at last!'

12

HOSTAGE

Johannes Gani strides through the storm towards the river, Captain Selim's rifle held in firing position. He has been ordered to bring in the girl. She ran towards the river: Greenboots will be escaping by boat.

'Shoot the boy. The girl and Mueller I want brought back here. Understand?' Even in his blood and agony Selim found the strength to fire orders, not least for the destruction of Old Ruiz' bar.

Gani is exhausted, hungry and utterly confused. He accepts, he is lucky: Selim was in too much agony, too haunted by a vision of dying from loss of blood to accuse him of neglect and incompetence.

And possibly worse, if Marquez' suspicions about Gani were to be considered.

Nothing has worked out. Everything has gone wrong; and Selim – horrible. A goner for sure. His men are laughing at him behind their hands: it will be the joke of the regiment, the joke of the year. One soldier made the first quip which will be followed by countless more, equally heartless, equally gloating: 'The captain'll have to piss out of his ears in future!'

They have called in the helicopter: will there be time?

Gani is in shock. And the girl: she too will be the talk of the regiment; and that talk will be building her up into something – a monster, a heroine, the wildcat of the forest?

Who knows? But this is for sure, the hunt for her will be unrelenting and merciless.

Gani admits to himself – I fancied her. What happened to Selim could have happened to me. Now she has the captain's revolver, a Browning. Old prejudices have returned: for all her book-learning, she's still a savage.

And yet, what courage! Which is what I'm short of at the moment. His fingers loosen on the Kalashnikov. With my luck, it's probably too wet to fire.

Lieutenant Johannes Gani has, in this vengeful storm, forgotten his orders and lost his resolve. He would like to lose himself in the storm, just lie there, shelter himself from the hacking rain.

I want to go home.

'Take men,' Selim had commanded. Two had obeyed – where were they now? She could be waiting for me in the trees by the river, Gani thinks. He halts. His feet are skating from under him. He is sliding, falling, skidding on mud towards the flooded bank.

Though the painter has been released, Old Ruiz' boat is reluctant to depart from its master's jetty. The rain blinds. The wind rushes waves into the boat. Hans Mueller's Doc Martens are awash. He is reluctantly holding the Browning while Lyana and Muyu attempt to unharness Ruiz' faithful craft.

'Why's she not moving?' The boat advances a metre, then appears to be tugged back to base. Hans reaches for an oar, thinking the boat is stuck against something submerged beneath the water.

Muyu shakes his head, climbs past Greenboots, lunges at a chain which, until this moment, has remained invisible; a chain firmly locked around a main spar of the jetty.

Lyana is first to spot Gani emerging from the last of the trees. He is aiming his weapon as if expecting to be ambushed. She thinks, how stupid he must be to come this way alone.

He is also clumsy. The slope below him proves ambush enough. It pulls his legs from under him. He is on his back. Nothing will stop him sliding straight into the river. His rifle, being lighter (and probably better designed) slides faster than he does.

For Gani, what can go wrong will go wrong. 'Hell!'

The Kalashnikov plummets into the river; and Gani follows with a bigger splash. He is up to his knees. He believes he might spot the rifle. When he glances up, he sees Hans Mueller aiming Selim's Browning straight at his head.

'Hands up!' Hans is actually grinning, for the phrase seems so daft. 'Hands up or you're a dead man.'

Greenboots may be joking: after all, he is supposed to be a pacifist. But there is such a thing as an accident; a trigger pressed as a result of shaky nerves or a nudged elbow. Gani has no will to test Greenboots' principles. He raises his hands.

'Now get on board – and no buts. Help him, Lyana. We don't want him crying all the way back to his captain about our little journey.'

The boat dips with Gani's weight, ships more of the wild river. 'Now sit!' orders Greenboots. 'You're a nuisance.'

Gani sits in the prow of the boat. He stares at his captors. He flinches at the sight of the dagger in Lyana's hand.

Meanwhile Muyu fights with the lock which holds the boat to the jetty. He grasps the stanchion. The wood is rotten. It is free of the walkway of the jetty, yet it will not agree to lean far enough for him to loop off the chain.

Lyana says, 'Shoot the lock.'

'Good idea. Another ten minutes,' says Greenboots, 'and I'd have thought of that myself.'

Muyu is about to climb out of the boat to raise the chain above the water level when the whole jetty collapses. The stanchions tip forwards and sideways. Planks spring from their housing of rusted nails, crashing over the boat.

One clouts Greenboots a broadside, tumbling him into the bottom of the boat. The Browning spins from his grasp. In that instant it is Gani's for the taking. Destiny, it seems, has not deserted him after all.

He stoops for the gun. It is below water in the boat but he is certain of the spot where it fell. Though his hand is scarcely centimetres away from the handle of the Browning, he will not make the distance.

His hair is grasped, head sprung back till he fears his neck is broken; and the dagger he knows has already wrought such damage is now at his throat. The hand that holds the dagger is the same one which has probably delivered Selim to his maker.

Does the blade still drip with Selim's blood?

'Please?' Pathetically he puts up his hands again.

Greenboots has dropped forward into the boat – but the vessel is free, charging into midstream, with Muyu fighting to do two things, grasp the tiller and ease Greenboots back into a sitting position.

Lyana's eyes pierce the night – with fury, with rage, or simply with callous intent? It hardly matters: she is a killer and Gani is at her mercy.

Yet she speaks softly: 'Promise?'

Gani is not sure what Lyana is demanding, though he guesses; he knows a promise may mean nothing under duress, but for the present it is the best tactic he can think of to save himself from a knife in the throat.

At least, he considers, that is where I would prefer it. He is remembering Selim's men, laughing. Hadn't another soldier said, 'The Butcher had best forget the dancing girls of Bali'?

No one will laugh at you, Lieutenant, if you are stabbed in the throat.

'I promise.' He sits back. He hates the water. The way it is looking, rising up and pitching over the sides of the boat, indicates that it feels the same about him.

The world hates me. He glares at Lyana. He thinks, And you I ought to hate most of all.

Greenboots is upright. The storm has lashed him into a pale dream of wakefulness. To all his woes, his aches and pains, his cuts and bruises, his fever, the night has added concussion. But it has also provided a bonus: in the plastic bag brought by Lyana, he has found a small piece of heaven – a half bottle of whisky.

'Bless you, my angel!' He has unscrewed the top, taken a gulp of heaven. He raises the bottle. 'And bless my old pal Ruiz!' His gaze turns towards the prisoner. 'You! Think yourself lucky there's not a bullet in your head for what's happened here today.'

The prisoner prefers to watch his enemy the river.

'Okay, concentrate on the flood, if you like, and remember: once upon a time this river buzzed with trade. All gone – the coffee, the sandalwood. Instead, you barbarians arrive, cut down the forest, turn the earth upside down in search of gold.'

The boat is in midstream. No need for the outboard motor. Steering is all that matters. Greenboots hates wet feet. That is why he bought his Doc Martens in the first place. He had boasted, 'The Docs protect against heat, cold, poison ants and spiders, snakes and they're strong enough to kick the hell out of Yellow Giants.'

Not true, of course. The Yellow Giants have triumphed; and now the river in the boat is trying to do the same. He snaps at Gani in the darkness. 'Bail us, soldier!'

Lyana unhooks a metal scoop from the side of the boat. She hands it to Johannes Gani. 'Please.'

He is amazed: this woman has shed the blood of an officer of the Indonesian occupying army. She will be the most hunted fugitive on the island. She can expect torture which will destroy for ever her youth and beauty. She will be taken out and when the soldiers have had their way with her she will be shot.

She knows this; must do. And here, a knife-point away, one bullet away, is a soldier with the evidence against her; who, in the event of Selim's death, will stand witness against her. Yet she says 'Please' to him.

Like Greenboots, Johannes Gani is afraid of water. He can swim a little, yet feebly. And if he did attempt to escape overboard, what then?

At least we're heading for the ocean and the town. Play it cool. Go along with things – survive; and then work out a strategy of escape. Gani, taking comfort from his thoughts, bails frantically, for the water in the sheets of the boat is washing against his calves.

For a second he glances up from his labours; could the girl be smiling at him? He is wheezing like an old man. An asthmatic, Johannes longs for his inhaler, left behind in the camp.

That smile: it is surely the one which enticed Captain Selim; for a moment – a tragic moment for him – she must have smiled to put him off his guard. He glares back at Lyana, as if to say, 'I remember!'

She is wondering how much I know; how much I will tell. You'd better do me in, lady. Saying what I know might rescue my career. Perhaps I am not finished yet. I've not, after all, lost my quarry: they are here, all three of them. Making it easy for me.

As Gani returns the water to where it belongs, the boat rises on the tide, moves faster than before; seems to float and fly. It is a kind of hell, yet also touched with magic: four figures lashed by the rain, one drinking and ranting on about how the ecology of the island is being destroyed, one with gaze fixed on the shifting course of the river, the other two – with nowhere else to look – watching each other.

Soon, perhaps, thinks Gani, sleep will find out the boy. Greenboots is already dozing. Then it will be me and the girl. It will be a trial not of strength but of patience. She will sleep eventually. Then I will act.

Greenboots is resting his head against Lyana's shoulder. His eyes open slowly, and he asks, drowzily, 'Just what did happen back there?'

Lyana's eyes are fixed on the storm-driven forest. Her lips are sealed, except for one word: 'Enough.'

13

UNWELCOME VISITOR

'These papers not valid.'

'Of course they're valid. I'm an Australian citizen.'

'Not valid, miss. You go back.'

'Go back where?'

'Go back Australia. You not wanted here.'

All the flight passengers have passed through to the tiny concourse of the island's airport except Emily Bryson, journalist.

'The second document you are mauling,' she insists, 'is an authorization – a permit. I am here to cover the United Nations Human Rights Commission investigation.'

'Sorry, you go back on plane.'

'So Indonesia's human rights abuses start here, do they – before you can even step out of the airport? Now please call your boss.'

'No boss. Me boss here. These papers not valid.'

A security button has been pressed. Two soldiers wearing green berets approach from the concourse. 'I am an Australian citizen!'

The official permits himself an indiscretion: 'You girlfriend of wanted man. Greenboots is criminal. You go back to Australia.'

'Criminal? How is Hans Mueller a criminal?'

Emily pulls out from her heavy shoulder-bag a pen and notebook. The pen is a miniature tape recorder. But the Green Berets have arrived. They await the order to manhandle her.

The official shoves a newspaper across the counter along with her closed passport. There is a picture of Hans on the front page. She is not given time to read the story, but the headline talks of an uprising of forest folk, led by the infamous Greenboots.

Soldiers have been killed.

The Green Berets are instructed to escort Emily Bryson back to the plane.

'Okay, okay. I go,' she says, falling into the manner of speech of the official. Green Berets are notorious. The prospect of being taken across the dark tarmac into no man's land is something Emily is determined to avoid.

'I demand a civilian official.' Her voice is raised. Passengers are taking an interest. 'Unless you are actually going to arrest an Australian citizen.'

The official wants an end to this little scene: Indonesia and Australia are friendly nations. There could be a fuss. This woman has been trouble before. The last time she attempted to visit the island with her camera and her notebook she had won an interview with the Red Bishop, an outspoken friend to the people. His call to the world to help liberate the island was published in papers as far afield as Lisbon and San Francisco, to the acute embarrassment of the government and the occupying forces.

She was never allowed to meet up with Hans. She was put on a ship, her camera and film confiscated.

'You go peaceful, then?'

'I go peaceful. But I shall report this to the high commissioner.'

A stewardess is called. 'Escort lady to plane – quick!'

Emily goes out through the swing doors with the stewardess. 'You believe in all this?' she asks. She has rolled up the newspaper. Now she flattens it out to protect her from the rain which at this moment is battering the fevered head of her lover many miles away.

The stewardess knows less English than the official, but she is more informative. 'Soldiers kill all island. Because of rebellion.'

'Rebellion?' Emily feels the storm is about to blow her off her feet. She shouts into the monsoon wind. 'What rebellion?'

'See paper.'

'Okay.' They are approaching the plane. The rain blinds them. At the foot of the steps up to the aircraft Emily holds out her hand, shakes that of the stewardess. 'I'll be all right. Thanks.'

She mounts the steps. The girl turns, runs for shelter. Because of the rainstorm, the steward who would normally be standing at the top of the steps to welcome passengers has retreated inside.

Emily Bryson suddenly turns on her heels. Who'll notice? My return ticket's not till Friday. She descends the steps. From where she has been standing high above the ground she could just make out the perimeter fence behind the runway lights. Beyond them is the wind-churned ocean; and below that ocean floor is oil – one of the reasons this brave little island might never win its independence from what Hans' friends in the forest call the Distant Masters.

Rebellion? And me leaving by plane? Not bleeding likely.

Emily ducks her head into the storm. She is being driven sideways, but she is thankful. For once, she thinks, Old Man Monsoon is on the side of the good guys. The fence is not far off. She can see the headland, and tucked inside its partial shelter, the lights of the town.

And if the fence is electrified, what then? Huh, the things I do for you, Hans Mueller.

Don't give me that, she imagines Hans replying. It's not me you want, but a juicy front-page story. What's all this about a rebellion: you're not in trouble again?

She is almost at the fence. There are tall floodlights which the force of the storm is swaying perilously. She forgets the risk of electrocution, holds the fence, leans against it. She is breathless. The storm is so fierce it hurts.

The paper reporting the death of Greenboots during the attack on the soldiers is torn out of her hands by the storm. She is to know nothing of how a so-called man of peace has insulted his tolerant hosts by stirring up the tribes of rebellion.

Such is the state of turbulence of the forest

people, continued the newspaper story, that the visit of the United Nations Commission might have to be postponed.

Indefinitely.

The word 'rebellion' sticks in Emily's mind; for with rebellion, even one faked by the authorities – which this probably has been – reprisals will follow.

In short, bloody vengeance; like the massacre at Santa Cruz.

She follows the route of the fence. Come on, Good Fairy, give me a break. Ahead, a gate leads out on to a quiet, single track road. It ought to be locked and bolted. But it isn't.

Careless. Emily guesses this must be the route the military uses to smuggle dope in and out. I got good headlines for the drug-running story (supplied by Greenboots' friends in town): CRACK KOPASSUS TROOPS IN COCAINE RACKET.

They'll never forgive me. Or Hans. Into Emily's inner ear comes advice from Greenboots: 'Find Sister Osario, she'll offer you shelter, no questions asked.' Emily remembers the instructions – ask for the quayside square with the statue of a missionary pointing out to sea. Then look for the chapel with a wooden steeple.

'Oh, and another thing.'

'Yes?'

'Make sure you're not followed. Security is everywhere.'

I've got your birthday present, Hans: best

Scotch, Cadenhead's 25-year-old blended Puta-chieside. Muyu Father will love it. We'll all sit under a tree and get plastered together.

There is no reply.

Emily closes the gate behind her. I've a second bottle to share with Old Ruiz, so long as he doesn't insist on playing me at chess.

Emily Bryson has visited the village of Muyu Father only through the window of Hans Muel-ler's letters, yet she feels she knows them as friends.

Muyu Father seems far too wise to start a rebellion. And you, Hans – well, you're too dis-organized. Emily smiles at the prospect of at last meeting the characters Hans Mueller may one day lovingly describe in his book: Old Ruiz taking half a day and a bottle of the hard stuff to make a single move on the chessboard; Muyu the young hunter captivated by the tales of Greek and Viking heroes Hans narrates around the night fire; and Lyana of the dark past, Hans' bright pupil.

Emily feels their friendship reaching out to her. She walks towards the lights of the town. To the storm she shouts, 'And you, you can blow all you like. If there's been a rebellion I'm going to report it!'

14

A GAME OF CAT AND MOUSE

While the storm has lasted there has been no need to start the engine of Old Ruiz' boat. The main thing is to steer clear of the bank. Muyu stares at the prisoner, not much older than himself. Gani opts to look gloomily, resignedly into the bottom of the boat, at the water still running to and fro over his feet.

Greenboots is fighting against sleep. He is thinking twice about the wisdom of allowing this intruder on board. 'What are we going to do with you, comrade?'

Lyana shares out food – rain-soaked biscuits, pickle, two bottles of beer. Catching Hans' eye, she gestures towards Lieutenant Gani.

'Have you eaten, soldier? No? Give him something, Lyana.'

She offers the prisoner the same fare as his captors. Hans decides talking might keep him awake. He says, 'I think these two friends of mine will want to ask you a few questions. They have lost their home, been driven out by you and your men. Their elders have been murdered. This young man's father was shot down merely for wishing to protect his people. Aren't you ashamed? Or do you just obey orders?'

The prisoner is silent.

'What harm have the forest folk ever done you Indonesians that you invade their island, eh? Still silent? I mean, what did they tell you all as you were brought a thousand miles from your own home to kill people you knew nothing about?'

Silence. 'Well, if we can't communicate – turn out your pockets. Come on.' Hans demands Gani's wallet, made of plastic, torn, its contents saturated.

'Pity it's so dark, we could spend a while looking at your photographs. Girlfriend, have you, in Jakarta?'

The prisoner shakes his head, stares hopelessly into space, prompting Greenboots to say, with equal feeling, 'How precious home is!' Then more sternly he adds, 'At least there will be a home somewhere for you to return to.' He hands back the wallet.

For a while Greenboots keeps his own silence. The boat seems to relish wider water. It slips through a mist thrown up by the storm. The wind has tired itself out. There is a split in the clouds above the trees and almost as a reminder that life can be beautiful, the moon casts a ripple of golden light across the forest.

Eventually Greenboots pronounces the prisoner's first name. 'Johannes? That is a Dutch name, is it not? Well, Johannes, it is likely we're going to have to kill you. If we let you go you'll run back to your captain and report our whereabouts.'

The soldier has been watching Lyana; so still, as if carved from the marble of the island. 'My captain is in no fit state to listen to my reports.' Gani looks hard at Lyana: will she not say something; admit it? She simply returns his stare, challenging him to add even a single word.

All at once the crew of Old Ruiz' boat are silenced by an engine roar overhead. A French Alouette helicopter cuts through the broken cloud above them, heading from the Sad Place to the city. Its light-beam races over the trees, probes the course of the river. Fleetingly it illuminates the four fugitives in their getaway boat.

Hans and Muyu instinctively duck. But Lyana glares up at the helicopter in defiance. She guesses at the purpose of this hasty flight to the capital. For the present at least, the girls of the forest will be secure from the mauling hands of the Butcher.

Gani cannot let the moment go, such is his own despair and disbelief. 'For what happened, there will be reprisals.'

'Tell us something new, soldier!'

Gani speaks words of accusation, his eyes on Lyana. 'A woman was seen. The weapon was a knife. The charge will be attempted murder or murder itself.'

He cannot move her. All he wants is for her to speak – for aren't they in a way partners? He knows her secret. One day she could owe him her life.

Greenboots is severe. 'I hope you're not suggesting, Lieutenant, that you were in some way a

116

witness.' Once more Gani seeks refuge in silence, in an averted gaze. 'Because if you were, we would have all the more reason to leave you at the bottom of this river.'

Gani cares for his life even though everything about it has gone wrong. He speaks the truth. 'I saw nothing.'

'But you know everything, is that it?'

For a brief second Gani senses Hans' anxiety. There is hesitation in his voice. The killing business is not what Greenboots is good at.

Gani's mind has been in shock, a lump of useless mud. Yet the mention of death by drowning has stirred the grey cells. He is in trouble, but his predicament can still – if his nerve holds – be turned to advantage.

After all, he reminds himself, you are a secret agent of the government; you have orders; and these apply directly to the man sitting opposite you in this boat.

Indeed here are three of the most wanted rebels on the island. You can still snatch glory from disgrace. Take them prisoner, bring them in alive or dead and you will once more be shaking hands with the president.

Better still, you will be given a posting away from this island of blood and of weeping. Father, will you then acknowledge that I have turned out a good son?

Gani produces a smile. His confidence is rising with every moment. All this has been a miserable farce for him, but it need not look like that. In hindsight, what has happened in the last twenty-four hours might be made out to be a brilliant strategy.

The weakness in his resolve is Lyana. She fascinates him, draws him away from himself to a self he scarcely recognizes. She has committed a monstrous crime yet seems to have left all memory of it to evaporate in the dying storm.

Gani hears himself say to Greenboots, 'I am not a bad person . . . In fact, it was through me your friends were able to rescue you. I called off the guards.'

'And why should you have done that?'

Gani leans a little to his left, taps the long pocket of his trousers. 'Your book, I think. I had never realized . . . the things that have gone on here. You see, in training they told us we had to clear out the Communists. That's what the native people wanted.'

Ever the optimist, Greenboots wants to believe this young man; and he is flattered that a book of his – banned throughout Indonesia – is nevertheless kept against all regulations by the young officer.

Gani feels encouraged. He recognizes too that Greenboots' head is swaying. Soon he will drop off to sleep. Who knows, then perhaps the others will do the same?

Keep talking.

'You see, the press back home, they tell us how good the army has made things on the island. New schools, health centres. What they don't tell us –' here Gani looks long and searchingly at Lyana – 'is that Bakasa is the only language allowed in the schools, not Tatum, the language of the island people.

'They told us how the government has opened clinics to help with birth control, yet you say in your book, Herr Mueller, that the plan was really to sterilize the women so they could not have babies.'

He sighs, and continues, 'Your account of the killings in the cemetery of Santa Cruz – that was so moving. It could . . . it could change a person.'

Greenboots' mind is not at its best. He is grateful to think that his writing might have won a convert. 'Yes, friends of mine died at Santa Cruz, students most of them, merely wishing to accompany a funeral. And then there were the survivors, taken to hospital – where they too were murdered by your people.'

'Not mine!' Gani's protest is heartfelt. 'Selim and his sort, maybe. I mean, in our papers they said nineteen died. Yet you claim in your book over two hundred and fifty were killed.'

Greenboots nods, unhappy to be reminded of an event during which his own life had been at risk, and he had been saved only by the boldness and quick thinking of a photographer called Steve Cox.

Steve's photographs of the massacre now flashed across Greenboots' inner eye. Horrible. 'To be precise, 271 lost their lives and 382 were wounded.' He is momentarily forgetting his fever, the head which beats with pain. 'But we continue to mourn the 250 still missing.'

Gani is convinced he is winning over the sick man. 'Back home they said that was propaganda. Yet what was worse was when they ran the trucks over the wounded in the hospital grounds.'

'True, true.'

'Crushed the heads of some protesters with rocks.'

'It's all there, my friend!'

'And then, as you say, they gave poison pills to the injured –'

'Paraformaldehyde –'

'Yes –'

'A lethal disinfectant normally used to kill insects.'

'Detestable!' Gani can no longer tell whether he means this, whether it is a sincere expression of revulsion or whether he is still playing the part of the heroic spy.

'Yes, as you say, Lieutenant, detestable. The pills caused a slow and agonizing death – internal bleeding and heart attacks.' Greenboots leans back so abruptly he seems for an instant to be in danger of falling out of the boat into the still-seething river.

Lyana steadies him. Her eyes search the face of the prisoner. It is a face of fear, of anxiety, of awful uncertainty – but is it also a face of treachery?

Greenboots is continuing, 'Such facts, my young friend, should convert you – make you one of us.' He decides it is time to test the prisoner for his sincerity. 'You nod. Do I take that to mean you are tempted?'

'Tempted?'

'You know what I mean. To reconsider your position.'

Gani still waits and Greenboots pushes further. 'In this war, as in all conflicts, you are for us or against us – agree?'

The lieutenant's mouth slowly shuts. He has perhaps talked too much; given Greenboots an advantage which he is plainly about to exploit.

'I think . . .' he replies, hoping the right thought will enter his head, 'given another chance – I'd be – have to be – neutral.'

'There is no such thing as neutral, Johannes. I am afraid at this moment you are not saying anything that will persuade me not to put a bullet in your head.'

Gani waits. Things, at last, had begun to go well. He has shown some cunning. Yet he has been too clever, not really thought ahead.

Greenboots is proposing, 'You could come with us to the capital and testify. Tell the authorities what really happened in the forest. About the murder of Muyu's people.'

Gani takes in all the faces of his captors. 'But they would shoot me before I could testify.'

'One bullet's as good as another.' Hans indicates the Browning in Lyana's hand. 'If you knew Lyana's life story, my friend, you would have no doubt whether she would use that gun.'

Gani needs no reminding of Lyana's resolve in

defending herself. Once more he has got himself in a fix. He raises his hands as if he has been captured for a second time. 'I will testify.'

And to himself, he says, I must escape.

Lyana has been watching Muyu. He is fighting sleep and sleep is winning. She nudges him. 'I'll steer.' He agrees, changes places with her, curls up on the middle seat of the boat. She wonders, will Muyu become one of those boys who haunt the docks, scavenging for survival; thieving, then falling into the hands of the soldiers?

Greenboots too has finally surrendered consciousness, though his knees still close tightly on the rucksack containing his precious log of the forest folk. If we do not get him to a doctor, he will die.

This part of the forest widens, almost into a lagoon. The boat slows, drifts, leaves a wave of gently folding ripples touched by moongold.

Lyana feels immeasurably sad: home gone, way of life abandoned, her adoptive people destroyed; and all that lies ahead is the town. It is this bleak vision of the future which, against her wish, presses the tears from her eyes; and these shame her, for the prisoner notices; gazes at her in astonishment.

Gani, in this instant, senses something other than his own desperation. The tears roll down the sky of her cheeks like miniature moons. He would like to reach out to her. Tears from a killer – is it possible?

His astonishment turns to amazement, for here are tears of his own; like hers, out of control, welling up, forcing him to gulp in air.

Why? Why now?

And she sees the tears. It can only make them laugh – something peculiar, unwanted, yet shared: the reason – what does it matter? He ventures into pale words: 'Funny, really . . . It's, well, it's just everything. You understand?'

Lyana nods; then having nodded, shakes her head. The gun is in her lap now, though Gani does not notice, does not want to notice. She spares him her thoughts: 'There is too much to understand.'

With his grimy hands Johannes Gani wipes away the tears. 'That's what I feel.' His words are genuine. He has never felt like this, never wept like this. He pauses, watches her. 'Will you be my friend?'

Her fingers do not, as he fears they might, reach for the Browning once more. Yet she is as calculating as he is. 'You wish to escape?'

He waits. He cannot believe his luck. He nods.

She smiles, then crushes his hopes. 'After you testify, Johannes. Then you may escape.'

15

BENNI WITH AN 'I'

'You want nice hotel?'

The youth on the autocycle has been following Emily Bryson for some time. The harbour road is longer than it looked.

He has drawn up on the road opposite her; scraggy, in shirt sleeves, drenched from the storm, but grinning.

'Have you been following me?'

'Very dangerous round these parts, ma-dame.' The youth glances ahead of him. Where the barbed-wire fencing of the airport ends, the town's overspill begins – makeshift huts with corrugated metal roofs, lean-tos, benders roofed with canvas. 'You get mugged, ma-dame. Dodge City very dodgy.'

The comment teases a smile out of Emily Bryson. 'Is that what they call it?'

'Also, City of the Lost.' Now the youth points up the road. 'No go that way, ma-dame. You catch nasty bullet – see, soldiers!' Lining the road are army trucks packed with newly arrived troops. 'Like you,' jokes the youth, 'no place to go!'

'What are you, a spy?'

The youth nods proudly. 'And bloody good

spy, yes, sir!' He waits. She waits. It's been a long day.

'Okay, then why don't you just scoot off to your bosses and report me?'

'You Aussie?'

'Yes, me Aussie.'

'I like your cricket, is great, man. I watch on telly. Mark Waugh, he the best. One day I visit big red rock – what you call it?'

'Ayers Rock.' Emily concedes she is stuck for the present with her companion. 'If I'm not to get shot, which direction would you advise?'

'You got camera?'

'Listen, I'm wet, hungry, tired and pretty fed up with things at the moment – are you going to help me or aren't you?'

'Spies not paid to help.'

Emily decides she will risk a mugging rather than a shooting. At the first sign of a track between the shanty houses, she turns inland. Her pet spy follows on his autocycle. 'No,' he says as she opts to take a left fork along a path deep in mud. 'Other way.'

'Look – what's your name?'

'Benni, with an "i".'

'Just what are your orders? To follow me or to turn me in?' Before he can answer, she adds, 'And whose side are you on anyway?'

Again he replies with relish and pride. 'Me spy both sides.'

'For the police?' He nods. 'And?'

'For Resistance.'

'You report one to the other?'

'Oh yes!'

Without her new friend Emily Bryson would be completely lost. The trails in Dodge City cross and loop and sometimes prove dead ends. Benni follows her patiently, always just a few wheel turns behind her.

'Ma-dame?'

'Yes, what is it now?'

He surprises her. 'You Greenboots' woman, correct?'

Why deny it? Benni with an 'i' seems to know everything. She plays him along. 'If you know so much, what have I got for Greenboots in this bag?'

Benni is solemn. He does not like being caught out.

'I'd better tell you, hadn't I, or you'll have nothing to report on me.' She reads Benni and his situation well. He appreciates this.

'Yes, you tell me – and I tell you where Sister Osario live. She put you up. You no go to hotel. Then you meet Chief.'

'Chief?'

'Chief of Resistance. Enrico Rosales – he my good friend.'

'The papers –'

'Say he also dead, right?'

'Alive after all – that's wonderful. The West thinks he was killed in an army ambush. The military even produced film of the bodies.'

'Enrico's friends, yes – but not Enrico.'

'Then there's still hope.'

'Soon, things change.'

'And does Enrico know you report to the police?'

'Of course. He tell me what to say.'

What this kid doesn't know isn't worth knowing. 'Sister Osario, you say?' An inner voice cautions her: all this could be a trap, a means to lure her into linking Greenboots with friends in the city. 'I thought she had been arrested.'

Benni is thoughtful for a moment. 'Always arrested. They no charge her. Beat her up, yes. After, they let her go.'

'Then they'll be watching her place?'

Benni points to himself. 'That my job tonight. Sister Osario my friend. She love the people.'

Emily remains suspicious and fearful. 'I don't want to disturb her, not at this hour of the morning. I'd best go to a hotel.'

Benni shrugs. He is curious. 'Why you not live with Greenboots? Have babies?'

'You'd better ask him.'

'He love island, eh, more than you?'

'About the same, I guess.' She cannot conceal her feelings. 'I don't want to give up my way of life, and he loves your people so much he won't desert them till they're free. That's the trouble with being in love with a hero.'

'I never meet him,' admits Benni. 'He handsome, and tall – like Clint Eastwood?'

'Afraid not. He's short – squat, some would say – and stinks of tobacco.'

'But he have great words, right?'

She is touched; at the same time she feels suddenly bereft and lonely. 'Yes, great words. Very persuasive.'

'I like you,' says Benni. 'You like me?'

She nods, smiles; there is a glimpse of dawn beyond the horizon of Dodge City and where the headland dips dramatically to the ocean. Now Benni moves ahead of Emily. The exhaust smoke from his machine is tinged with the pale crimson of morning.

'What is your name?'

'Emily.'

'We friends, yes?'

'Yes, okay, we friends.'

'And you journalist, correct?'

'Correct.'

'Then, Emily, you tell world. The Bapaks have more bad plans. You heard of Fence of Legs?'

Emily shivers, not with cold but with remembrance. The *pagar betis* or fence of legs had been, for the military, the final solution in the war against the island resistance. People had been dragged from their towns and villages to form a vast human chain supervised by the army.

Those who refused to become links in the chain or attempted to escape from it were shot. And this chain progressed metre by metre across the island, converging on the plains of Manatuto in the north corner of the island: its purpose, to trap every surviving member of the Resistance; as Colonel Fario had instructed his officers, 'To purge the island of the last of the vermin!'

The campaign was named, among other things, *Operasi Kikis* – final cleansing. And in darkness, the islanders let through their fence of legs the fighters of the Resistance; though at great cost to themselves. The army provided them with neither food nor drink and hundreds suffered fatal diarrhoea. They were left to die in the forest.

The operation ended not with the extermination of the Resistance but, in the words of Hans Mueller in his book, the 'massacre of the innocent'. In the region of Aitana ten thousand people, including babies, were slaughtered.

'They wouldn't dare try that again!' Emily exclaims.

Benni stares at his new friend. She is older but he is wiser. 'And who will stop them – the British, the Yanks, you Aussies? Pah!' It is Benni's turn to tremble a little, this time with rage. 'No, in Timor Sea – much oil. So you all keep quiet. Like Sister Osario say, you all like Mr Pharisee. When he see wounded man bleed, he cross street.'

There is to be more rain. Emily is too tired to argue. 'Okay, Mr Preacher. Sermon's over. Either lead me to shelter or report me to the authorities.'

Benni grins. 'You bet – I do both!'

16

SENTRY DUTY

The prisoner has asked for water. The salt tang of the ocean on the forest wind signals that the journey will soon be over. The future beckons with an unsmiling face. Lieutenant Gani has watched Lyana through the small hours. He senses her increasing uncertainty.

I must escape. If that helicopter was taking Selim to hospital then the whole army of occupation will be on red alert. The captain will demand revenge: my captors are dead meat. And so am I unless I can get away.

I must gain this girl's trust; make her my friend.

To begin his campaign for freedom, in a soft voice Gani asks, 'School – have you never been to school?' He pauses as she hesitates. 'Lyana? That is a beautiful name.

'School?' he repeats, taking a single swig of the bottle, wiping the top and politely returning it. 'You two, go to school?' No reply, only the harsh slap of the river against fallen trees. 'Everyone should go to school. That is government policy.'

He is surprised when Lyana answers him. 'Yes, in my village there was a school. The Bapaks came. Took our teacher away. Shot him in the bush. And when they returned they burnt the school. They took the people to a high place –'

'I don't want to know!'

'You asked and therefore you must be told.' The gun in her hand seems, in its silent power, to say 'Listen!'

'You and your people must be reminded again and again and for ever of the crimes you have committed against us ... Yes, all but a few children of the village were taken ... to the cliff above the river. They were made to stand along the edge –'

'It is not my fault –'

'I can still hear the sound of the machine-gun.'

'It's wrong to blame me – I've never killed anyone.'

'But you will.'

'Look at me!' A touch of self-pity colours his words. 'I'm a prisoner. My own people will think I'm a coward or a deserter. I'm less trouble to this island than a mosquito.'

Lyana relents: his helplessness moves her. Even Bapaks can be human. Gani feels encouraged to put his own case, his vision for a united, prosperous Indonesia. 'Surely we must all pull together, Lyana.'

She waits. She witnesses his own schooling; it oozes out phrase by phrase.

'You see, the future. I mean, your ways, Lyana – the tribal ways. Good grief, this is the twentieth century, nearly the twenty-first. There's got to be progress.'

She puts the words into his mouth. 'You think we do not move with the times?'

He does not see the trap. 'Exactly . . . So there have to be schools, and they must all speak the same language so we can feel one people. And learn the same culture. And there must be work, not idleness.'

'The forest people hunt – that is their work.'

'I mean jobs – jobs that earn money. So that you can spend, buy things.'

'And live in cities?'

'No. Yes. But –'

'In the factories, all day, with no view of the trees? Why?'

'Because to be wealthy our people – all our people – must trade and we must have something to trade with, like timber.'

'Our people trade. They have traded since the beginning of time. But they have not cut down the forest, for Mother Forest has given us life.'

Gani cannot grasp the thoughts which might overturn her argument. He speaks bitterly, threateningly. 'The bulldozers – your Yellow Giants – will not take No for an answer, Lyana. It's the way things are going. Adapt or die.'

'And if we do, what then?'

'You will be given houses, with roofs, with running water and electric light. You'll have jobs. You'll have radios, TVs, videos. You'll be able to find out what's going on in the big wide world.'

He is convinced that at last his point is hitting

home. He glances about him at the water-shining logs, the tree creepers, the glistening moss – a world to him full of menace and ugliness.

'It's time to change,' he says. 'And I could help you. I have contacts in the capital. You could even go to college one day, in Jakarta. Wouldn't you like that?'

She offers him no comfort. 'I would like my island to be free.'

He is desperate. 'Do you know, they're even digging for gold in the mountains. Big companies from overseas. The wealth in those hills could be colossal. And you think the government in Jakarta will give all that up?'

'Not willingly. But one day it must.'

Gani ignores Lyana's comment, brushes it aside. 'And another thing, tell me honestly, from your heart – what good has this Greenboots brought your people? Has he saved your forest home?' Johannes Gani shakes his head.

'No, all he has done is meddle. He's come thinking he is a great hero. All he's ever done for you is give the forest folk a bad name. He's stirred you up to rebellion. By doing so he has brought death and destruction upon your people.

'In truth, he is your enemy!'

At first Gani thinks Lyana has not been listening, then suddenly he is alert, tense, his pulses hammering in his neck. Sleep has proved more persuasive than his words.

Lyana's head has gradually, fitfully, come to rest on the shoulder of the arm which controls the boat's tiller. The gun in her other hand lies across her lap. Her finger is free of the trigger.

Wait. Just a minute or two more. With that gun in my hand I could bring home three prisoners. Greenboots to trial, why not? Then Gani remembers his orders. He is torn: there could be glory back home for the hero who captured an enemy of the state. Yet his career would be finished.

So, what's my alternative – to enter the capital a prisoner, covered with shame, forced to testify to the massacre? Either that or I grab the gun – take the risk of waking all three of them; and then what?

Must I kill them? It will be only a matter of time before they are captured and executed. He stares at Lyana. No, not her. In another time and another place, Lyana, who knows how friendship might have grown?

Perhaps. But we are too different. And there is no time to change. Gani chooses the third alternative. He must slip overboard without being seen. And it must be now. The sun will soon be on their faces. They will wake; and then I am truly finished, for the capital's probably only a couple of hours' distance.

Johannes Gani turns his head towards the still-dark shore. He shifts his hands from his knees to the sides of the boat; waits. Sleeping beauties. Pity the woman who marries Greenboots: his snoring is enough to wake the birds of the forest.

The prisoner sits upright. His hands tighten and thrust him slowly upwards. He must not tilt his weight to either side of the boat. He is almost standing now. He watches the swift motion of the river. Good, the boat is close to shore. There could be a collision with the far bank in a few moments, then his captors would have no need of an alarm clock.

He is over the side. The shock of the cold river, fresh from the high mountain, makes him gasp. His clothes are dragging him down and the current is too strong for his unpractised breaststroke. He is almost on the point of calling out, appealing for help.

Life counts for more than pride, even for Lieutenant Gani, but at the last moment his feet touch ground. The trailing fingers of a fallen tree meet his. Ripples choke him. He is rising from the water, and coughing; and without intending it, signals to anyone capable of hearing him the imminent disaster facing Old Ruiz' boat.

Mother Forest is rustling her branches, whispering a curt warning to her children: wake up before it is too late! Yet sleep is deeper than the river. Gani climbs the bank, coughing still. He hears the crash, prow against the trunk of a fallen tree, scraping submerged rock, swinging violently into the bank.

The lieutenant ducks for shelter. They could drown. And if they don't, I'll be to blame, not the river. I should have warned her. After all, she liked me. In time I might have been able to make her trust me.

Too late. He turns. The less I know, the better.

He runs up the sloping shoulder of the forest. He is free; and he is miserable at the prospect. He glances once more down towards the river.

I have never felt like this. For the briefest instant he senses Mother Forest has found words for him. He pauses, listens. A great truth seems to descend upon him, yet he can make no sense of it; except to answer the forest back, with one word: 'Lyana!'

17

SHIPWRECK

Muyu is fitfully rising from other waters – of a dream of Yellow Giants. There are as many now as the trees they have destroyed. The hills are bald and dry. Nothing grows on them; and Muyu Father is saying, Only one thing can save our people, my son. And Muyu is desperate to learn what this one thing can be, yet the voice of Muyu Father is too faint and the roar of the Yellow Giants too great for the message to be heard.

He is awake, yet now he dreams the words: 'You must return with help, Muyu son.' He hears the river. The sun is lodged and burning in the trees above him. He opens his eyes, sees Lyana slumbering, cries out, for the river bank is rising up to attack him.

'Lyana!'

Too late. Old Ruiz' boat hits a cliff of black mud. Muyu hurls himself against Lyana, attempting to reach the tiller, but in her own dream there are monsters. She fights him off and her strength is equal to Muyu's.

The rudder is free, swinging at the whim of the river. The darkness is splintered with light. The prisoner, thinks Lyana, is struggling for the gun.

'No!' She thrusts Muyu away, recognizing

her friend only as Old Ruiz' boat strikes half-submerged logs, its prow rising above them, tilting, then violently capsizing in still waters beneath the overhanging bank.

Hans Mueller is pitched overboard. The boat has righted itself, but the danger has increased: the outboard motor is still running; and Hans' point of entry into the river is now concealed by the boat.

Muyu has no word in his language for 'propeller' but he understands well enough how this one could cut his friend Greenboots to pieces.

Lyana has leapt into the river, attempting to secure the boat against the fallen tree which helped rescue Johannes Gani.

'He's gone!'

Could the prisoner too be drowning?

Muyu dives. The cold burns his eyes, open despite the blackness. But sight is in his hands. He touches Greenboots. He cannot hold him; and all at once both are being carried, choking, down river.

Lyana has looped the boat's painter to the fallen tree. She scrambles over the two seats towards the outboard motor. Only now does she note how red the water is, as if the great river is bleeding to death. It is red with shale washed from the high ground and is now silting up.

It will be the mines.

Concealed in the woods above, Johannes Gani returns to the vantage point he has just abandoned. He is undecided: the old Johannes would have kept his fingers crossed that this accident would prove fatal. A drowned Greenboots would be just what Colonel Fario ordered.

Instead, Gani accuses himself: 'Deserter!' He watches Lyana seize one of the oars of the boat. She is scrambling along the river bank. Johannes can see the boy now, his arm crooked, hands grasping Greenboots under the chin, holding him up into the air.

It's my duty to get back to base and report their arrival. The voice of duty is strong. It mimics Captain Selim: 'Correct?'

Lyana skids down the bank on her heels. She calls Muyu. He is battling against the current, but Lyana has pressed ahead to where there has been a landslide. The whole forest here seems to have toppled from the near-precipice above. It's the red shale again.

The forest no longer exists on this side of the river. It has been cleared and the clearing now forms a new river, coming down from the mountain – a river of red sludge.

She is holding out the oar to Muyu and Greenboots but her feet are sinking in the sludge. 'Can't reach!'

Muyu has seen the narrowing of the river. For a second he had lost his grasp of Greenboots, felt a hand in his face, jerking his head back, but now he has circled behind the drowning man, grabbing him by the hair.

The red mud is up to Lyana's knees, sucking her downwards. 'Won't be beaten!' She drops the oar. With her hands clasped beneath her thigh she wrenches her leg from the angry mud.

She moves, heaves. The oar hovers a fingerspan from Muyu's grasp.

'Again!'

Hans makes the difference. He has recognized that Muyu is his friend, not Gani sent to murder him – as his fevered dream foretold. He co-operates, allows himself to be pulled through the water on to the red shale.

He spits water. His glasses are gone, and with them, his sight. They roll him on his side and the rest of the river dribbles from his mouth. The sun is on him. His clothes steam. And all Hans Mueller can think about is – 'The rucksack – Lyana, my rucksack, my log!'

She leaves Muyu to nurse the near-drowned Greenboots. Hans' log is as precious to Lyana as it is to him. She reaches the boat, neatly at anchor. That rucksack also contains whisky to revive Greenboots, food to sustain him, but if the log is lost so too will be Hans' will to live.

'What I have written,' he had once confessed, 'is what I am. I know you understand that, Lyana.'

'It's lost, it's gone!' cries Greenboots to Muyu. 'Well?' he shouts as Lyana approaches, tugging Old Ruiz' boat by the painter.

'That was very clever of you, Hans.'

'Clever? Me?'

'You stuck it under the seat.' She holds up the rucksack, soaked and dripping, but with all its contents intact.

Greenboots sighs, a little ashamed of his tantrum. 'I dreamt that Gani had stolen it. Published it under his own name.' His joy abates: 'My glasses. Without them, life's a blur.'

He strains to make out the figures in front of him: 'Gani?'

Muyu speaks for Lyana. 'The prisoner is gone.'

Having abated, Greenboots' joy now fades utterly. 'Gone? Not drowned?' He allows himself to be helped back into the boat.

Lyana waits for his judgement. She confesses, 'I fell asleep, Hans. All this is my fault.'

'Then he is free?'

'Forgive me.'

'Forget it, child. If anyone's to blame it is me.' He pauses. The fever has returned. He is swaying, shivering. 'It was my decision to spare Gani's life. And why? Because he flattered me, talked me into thinking what I'd written actually meant something to him.'

'Perhaps it did.'

'No. He used his brains. He fooled me.'

Lyana wants to say, 'And me too,' but Hans Mueller is deaf to all blame except his own. 'Our cunning little spy knows where we are and where we're heading – and that knowledge could mean a medal for him and the death of us!'

18

FAREWELL, MOTHER FOREST

Muyu is asking, 'Will Greenboots die?' Lyana holds Hans against her knee, his head crooked in her arm; and she feeds him as she would a baby or one of the sacred pigs of the forest folk.

His mind is a swarm of bees. 'Listen!' They listen. All he can hear is the buzzing in his head. 'Who is it?' Lyana does not bother to answer. She soothes Hans' forehead, dampens it once more. 'Osario – Sister Osario. You must find her. She will take us to Rosales, to the Resistance.' These few words leave him breathless. 'Am I dying, Lyana?'

His mind drifts, a broken branch on the river, twisting, tangling, one moment submerged, the next reaching into light. His mind has slipped back an hour. He thinks Lieutenant Gani is still on board. 'They will listen to you, soldier.'

Lyana's gaze meets Muyu's questioning eyes.

'You see, your testimony . . . it could be so important.'

Lyana's silence restores Greenboots to the present. He opens his eyes, counts his companions, two blurred shapes in a shaft of sunlight. 'Gone – our witness?' He struggles to recover his spirits. 'Bad, bad. Gani was our surety. Our passport . . .

And the Commission would have listened to him.'

Greenboots' head drops in despair for a moment. 'And he was almost in the bag – you noticed that, Lyana?'

'In the bag?'

'Converted – to our cause.'

'You think so?'

'You doubt it?'

'He talked to save himself. He would have forsworn us soon enough.'

Greenboots is stubborn. 'I liked him. Misguided, but not wicked.'

Lyana is angry, in part with herself, in part with Greenboots who sees good in all people to the point of letting them harm him and those he wishes to protect. 'He is a Bapak – and a soldier.'

'Not all Indonesians are bad, Lyana.'

'Indonesians who occupy our land – they are bad.'

Muyu has no doubts. 'He will betray us. The soldiers will be waiting by the river.'

'Then I suggest you leave me. Go back to the forest. All I have to offer you is the risk of arrest and torture.'

Lyana puts Hans Mueller's petulance down to his injuries and his sickness. 'No, Greenboots – you know that cannot be. There is no purpose any more but this. And have you forgotten? Our people lie unburied in the forest.'

She fishes in the rucksack, unscrews the half-bottle of whisky, hands it to him. 'You, Greenboots, must testify.'

143

He drinks, hears Lyana add coaxingly, 'And Emily, won't she be there, waiting for you?'

Hans brushes thinning hair from his eyes. 'Of course – Emily with my birthday present. I need to smarten up. Grief – my glasses!' The forest looks to him like a painting whose colours have drained into each other. Vertical strokes of green cut through horizons of rust red and morning blue.

He jokes, 'Do you reckon there's a decent optician in town?'

The river has grown wide, less friendly. Gradually Mother Forest is releasing the silent voyagers from her protection. Ahead, white birds skim the water then rise swiftly up beyond the trees, becoming almost golden against the sky.

In the boat, the sick man sleeps. Muyu looks to Lyana to tell him of the future. 'At the coast,' he begins, and then breaks off.

Now she speaks her thoughts. 'Greenboots is right. We must not hate all the Bapaks for what a few of them do to us.'

'No? I do.'

Lyana says, 'I guess you are right. The lieutenant would not have spoken for us. Yet he was troubled.'

'Troubled?'

'Sad – like us, struggling to understand things.'

Muyu is amazed. 'He killed our people.'

'Perhaps not him.'

Muyu senses Lyana's distance from him. Something happened: in the dark night under the moon, enemies had met. They had talked. In the dark night under the moon perhaps the young man had cast a spell on his captor. 'What did he say to you?'

'He said all things must change.'

'And what did you say?'

'I asked him why.' Muyu waits; yet Lyana offers no further explanation. 'We disagreed. And that is an end of it.'

Long before the river widens into the estuary, the capital's outlying suburbs – called Tin Town – begin. There is precious little tin, except corrugated sheeting for roofs or patches for plaster walls. Many of the shacks are built on stilts over the water. They are assembled from anything that might keep out the wrath of the monsoon – woven cane, packing cases, abandoned car doors, oil drums.

Along the shoreline women wash clothes and exchange the gossip of the morning. Children splash and shout in the shallows amid dark rainbows of petrol and knee-deep refuse. Soon there are more permanent structures – moorings, warehouses, loading bays, two-storey stone and brick buildings rising above the makeshift huts of the immigrants.

There is harbouring, cranes, trucks, noise. Beyond the rim of the river there are glimpses of fine houses, white and pink-washed, and these continue up into wooded hills. Skilful navigation has become necessary: motor-launches pass, their backwash rocking Old Ruiz' little boat; and the rocking, rather than casting Greenboots into a deeper sleep, wakes him.

He is refreshed, almost his old self. The city is another blur, but the sounds alert him: far off, a plane is landing. There is the distant murmur of motor traffic. 'Lyana, tell me what I ought to be seeing.'

Lyana describes a woodyard stacked high with timber.

'Our trees?' wonders Muyu.

'Then it's not far – look out for a tiny island in mid-river. I holed up there after the massacre at Santa Cruz. It's opposite a sort of warehouse on stilts. Can you see it?'

'The river curves here – yes.'

'Trees growing out of the water,' observes Muyu.

'Don't worry, there's enough dry land and shade to hide us till dark.'

They close in on the islet. It is scarcely thirty paces across. 'We shall need food,' says Lyana. 'And more water.'

Muyu is puzzled. He points to the river. 'Water?'

Greenboots answers for Lyana. 'I'm afraid this water's full of dead rats, Muyu. I wouldn't put my big toe in it, never mind drink it.'

Muyu steers Old Ruiz' boat alongside the island and into welcoming shade. He jumps ashore, secures the painter to a sapling at the water's edge.

In action, Muyu knows himself; in action, he finds purpose: 'You will rest, Greenboots. And I will bring water and food.'

'Whatever you do, you do together – understand?' says Hans Mueller as he is eased on to his feet. But for the support of his companions he would crash on to his face in muddy grass. 'You see – fit as a fiddle!'

Lyana decides Hans must rest here, gather his strength. If they cannot bring a doctor to treat him, they will bring medicine to control his fever. 'How shall we find Sister Osario, Hans?'

'As easily as Security does! So take care. Friends usually wait till the spies have gone off for their Coke and chips.' He points down river. 'You must look out for a statue on the quayside. A missionary holding a Bible in one hand and trying to stop pigeons crapping on his head with the other.

'Then, cross the square – mind the cycle-taxis, they don't look where they're going. Down a side-street you'll see the spire of a wooden church. Go through into a courtyard. There's one door. Knock three times followed by two – and say Greenboots needs a new pair of specs.'

19

AWKWARD QUESTIONS AT THE RESIDENCY

In his gracious, high-ceilinged office in the residency of the governor, Colonel Fario of the Island Command has granted a press briefing to journalists who have flown in from Australia. He is assisted by Mr Hindarto, the governor's press officer.

Things are not going smoothly.

'If everything in the garden is as rosy as you claim it to be, Colonel Fario, why is it that despite my visa your officers tried to put me back on the plane last night?'

'Your name, madam?'

'And why is it that on a visit to an old friend in the city, I discover that she has been taken in for questioning for the third if not the fourth time in a month?'

'Your name, madam, if you please? And to whom are you referring?' Mr Hindarto, a small man, precisely and expensively dressed, has so far remained cool as well as smart. But questions the journalists have been firing at the colonel concerning the murder of civilians, torture and the deportation of hundreds of 'troublemakers' have loosened his temper.

Worse, such impertinent inquiries – pure hearsay – have resolved Colonel Fario not to utter another word.

'My name is Bryson, Emily Bryson, reporting for Survival International and the London *Independent*. And I am referring to Sister Osario.'

'You witnessed her arrest personally, did you, Miss Bryson?'

'No. She had already been taken.'

'Then you have no evidence that Sister Osario is not away in the Catholic quarter ministering to the sick. Tell me, madam, who was your informant?'

Emily has no intention of splitting on Benni spelt with an 'i'. She pursues her case. 'Her door was wide open, as if she'd been forced to leave in a hurry.'

'An emergency, no doubt. Perhaps a baby to deliver. We all acknowledge round these parts that Sister Osario is a Christian saint.'

Emily Bryson will not be talked down. 'If she was called to deliver a child, why should the benches in her chapel be overturned – and why was there blood on the step?'

Mr Hindarto concedes a point. He knows the Green Berets are often over-zealous in their duties; and Sister Osario is notorious for talking back to people, even those carrying guns. 'I assure you, Miss Bryson, the matter will be looked into.'

'Comarca prison, is that where she's been taken, Mr Hindarto, where the military conducts its systematic torture?' Emily turns her fury on the silent

Colonel Fario. 'All night your men have been rounding people up. Have they also been taken to Comarca, or is it so full you're having to use the warehouse at San Tai Ho?'

This lady is too well informed.

The colonel's eyes are concealed by dark glasses, a model even more fashionable and expensive than Captain Selim's Ray-bans, but the movement of his fingers on the desk betrays his anger.

'Will you confirm,' Emily Bryson continues, 'that the only citizens of this town we journalists will be permitted to talk to – and the only ones the members of the United Nations Commission will be allowed to interview – are soldiers disguised as civilians?'

Mr Hindarto despairs of Colonel Fario saying anything even under provocation. He glances, as if pleading for help, at the portrait of the nation's president hanging above the marble fireplace.

Seemingly unimpressed by the performance of the governor's press officer, the president offers neither comfort nor assistance.

Mr Hindarto now stares for a moment out of the tall windows of the residency towards the ocean. He does not like westerners. He does not like the lip of Australians; and Australian women with lip he finds particularly offensive.

If he could be granted one wish he would dispatch the lot of them over the balustrade at the bottom of the residency gardens – a sheer drop of some fifty metres. Yes, boot them off 'the governor's precipice' as it is called; and hey presto, no more awkward questions.

The absence of a fairy godmother to grant Mr Hindarto his dearest wish leaves him no alternative but to continue his brief: 'The four members of the Commission will arrive at the airport tomorrow at midday. The press will be permitted one hour, after which time the Commissioners will proceed to villages in the island where they will be free to talk to anyone they please.'

Emily spoils things once more: 'Will they be permitted to talk to Hans Mueller, nicknamed Greenboots?'

'Yes, Greenboots – where is he, why isn't he here?' This from a German reporter.

Again, Emily takes the lead. 'I am under instructions from Survival International not to return from this island until Hans Mueller's prize has been awarded to him in person.'

'Prize? I have not been informed of such a thing.'

'That is because your government has objected to the prize, refusing as it does to accept that the timber companies are destroying the island's forest.'

'That is nonsense, Miss Bryson.'

'Will Greenboots be permitted to receive the prize, for his work in defending both the forest and the people of the forest, or won't he?'

In Emily's shoulder-bag there is a second prize for Hans Mueller – the best malt whisky her salary could buy. 'We want a ceremony, with pictures to show to the world.'

This comment proves too much for Colonel Fario's patience. He barks, 'No ceremony!' Then he retreats swiftly into the silence of his dark glasses.

It is a tactical error which Mr Hindarto seeks to head off with a worse one: 'We know nothing of the prize you refer to. And to discuss the matter in present circumstances is quite out of order.'

'What circumstances, Mr Hindarto?'

After a glance at Colonel Fario, Hindarto answers, 'Our information is that Hans Mueller was killed in the high forest, leading a rebellion of local tribes.'

'Where's his body?' calls out one photographer. 'Show us the proof!'

Hindarto continues as though uninterrupted. 'Mueller was leading an attack on the workers of a timber company. Many were killed. His body will be produced in due course.'

Emily Bryson shakes her pen as if it were a spear aimed at Fario's heart. 'Hans Mueller is a pacifist. Everyone knows that! He would never take a life – never!'

Colonel Fario surfaces once more from his icy depths. 'You would of course have this information, Miss Bryson, as you are known to be Mueller's woman.'

Hindarto recognizes that Colonel Fario may have won a strategic victory. He interrupts, 'Yes, indeed, Miss Bryson. I think that what the colonel is suggesting is that you could well be an accomplice of Hans Mueller in his criminal activities.'

The portrait of the president seems now to smile down upon his faithful subject, and urge him on. 'Which, if I may return to your original question, explains why you were turned back at the airport.'

Hindarto is triumphant.

'Then why haven't I been arrested?'

Colonel Fario permits himself the smallest of smiles. 'Because, Miss Bryson, we are not in the business of abusing human rights in this country or interfering with the full flow of information required in a proud democracy.

'We have nothing to hide from the world's press, or from the Commission.' Fario too glances up at the portrait of his president. 'Nothing to hide!'

The president smiles his approval.

'Okay, so if Greenboots suddenly comes back from the dead, will he be given the chance to talk to the Commission?'

It has been reported to Colonel Fario that Hans Mueller escaped in the forest. There is a rumour that Greenboots knows of the Commission. He is the sort of man who would move heaven and earth to speak out on behalf of the forest people. For this reason Colonel Fario has put the entire army of occupation on the alert.

However, his earnest hope is that Lieutenant Johannes Gani, son of a general, will have faithfully and efficiently carried out his orders.

The colonel's voice is strained and harsh. 'Everything is possible, of course.'

Emily pushes her luck even further. She advances towards Fario's desk. 'And Rosales, the leader of the Resistance, will he be given the chance to address the Commission?'

Fario's control slips, to reveal the menace which has terrified the local population. He pounds the desk with his fist and the glass lodged over the carafe of water rattles. 'There is no Resistance! It was wiped out years ago. Absolutely – every man, woman and child!'

There is a terrible silence, broken eventually by Mr Hindarto's forced cough. 'Sir, I think –'

Emily baits the tiger, prods it with yet another question. 'Are you claiming, Colonel, that Rosales does not exist?'

'Rosales was burnt alive in his own house. No one could have survived that fire.'

'Did your men start it?'

Another journalist wields a sharp stick of words: 'But if Rosales suddenly came back to life, Colonel –'

'There is no Rosales. No Resistance!'

Mr Hindarto desperately tries to rescue his boss: 'The people are happy – it's only a few trouble-makers.'

'Happy?' cries Emily Bryson. 'Have you looked into the faces of the island people? Happy?'

No one has ever attempted such an onslaught on Colonel Fario, much less a woman. His chin juts out. He stands. He shakes his fist at Emily. 'You!'

'Yes, Colonel?'

'Had better take care, madam.'

'Is that a threat?' She turns to the other pressmen and photographers. 'Hear that, comrades?'

Colonel Fario is almost away, out of the room.

'One last question, Colonel,' shouts Emily. 'Is it true what they're saying in the town – that there's to be another Fence of Legs?'

Mr Hindarto closes his eyes. The president is scowling down at him as if he, the governor's underpaid, overworked press officer, was personally responsible for this disastrous briefing.

'That, lady and gentlemen,' he says, his voice choked, betraying a tremor of fear at the rage he will be treated to by Colonel Fario once they are behind closed doors. 'That concludes the business of the morning.'

'And the Fence of Legs?' persists Emily Bryson.

'Thank you.'

20

WANTED FOR MURDER

For Muyu the city is another forest, yet one that is strange and forbidding. It is the difference between forest and jungle: the one friendly, its pathways known, its mysteries familiar; the other hostile, its pathways a confusion.

Streams, heavily polluted with waste, join the river at this point. Dams of rubbish have been forced open by last night's storms and scattered along the shoreline. The shanty houses have produced alleys and eventually spaces recognizable as streets.

People and vans, people and delivery trucks jostle together. Becak drivers steer their three-wheel taxis between street vendors; and below the houses on either side are rows upon rows of market stalls. There is food to be had, but only in exchange for coins and Muyu has never possessed a coin, or needed to. The food reminds him of how hungry he has become. He hears Lyana say, 'Greenboots needs food.'

'I will ask,' says Muyu innocently. In the forest, to ask is to be given. When he steps towards one of the stalls Lyana tugs him back. But he is proud. He addresses the stallholder of a barrow laden with fruit and sweet potatoes. 'Please, I am starving!'

The stallholder glares at the forest boy. 'Then go and dig up some roots, kid. This is business, not a charity.' He looks at Lyana. 'You get your grubbly little brother out of here, darlin', or I'll call Security.'

He stares past her. The market is under surveillance, with Green Berets stationed riverside and townside and mingling with the crowd.

Lyana does not ask for food. 'I am sorry,' she says. 'He is my cousin. He is new here. Could you please tell us where the statue is – the one of the missionary?'

There is to be no time for an answer. Prompted by hunger, provoked by being treated like a wicked child, Muyu takes action. After all, he is the chief of his tribe; and chiefs don't beg. While the stallholder's attention is fixed on Lyana, Muyu advances on the fruit. He seizes a huge bunch of black grapes, at the same time thrusting his other hand into a neatly stacked mountain of satsumas. The mountain collapses, backwards over the stallholder, forwards on to the market ground.

'Thief! Stop the thief!'

Lyana is following her friend. The sight of the spilled satsumas has suddenly brought other kids – starving too, perhaps – swarming around the stall. Pushing becomes shoving. Shoving becomes fighting. The barrow overturns. All the stallholder's fruit and vegetables pitch and roll over the wet cinder ground.

'Officer! Officer – thieves!'

All the world is a thief; and the real thief and

157

his accomplice are sprinting towards a gap between the shanty houses. He is not fast. His limp is plain to witness; and the crowds notice. They too call to Security.

Boy with a limp! Boy with a limp!

Lyana is amazed at him. She is calling after him but he is deaf to her warnings. He is a fool. She will tell him that when she catches up with him. He has probably ruined everything. She will tell him that too. Yet at the same time she cannot resist a feeling of admiration.

In an alleyway and in shade, Muyu halts, squats down. He does not speak. Makes no excuse. He hands her a satsuma and a share of the grapes. He does not seem to care that the Green Berets may be coming along this way at any moment.

For a while at least he has triumphed over the city which ignored him, which responded to him with disdain. 'Muyu Father says, all nature's fruit belongs to the people who need it.'

For Lyana there is too much to say, so she says nothing.

'And,' continues Muyu, 'he told me of the big city – beware! The spirit is darkened when too many people live together like this. Bad things happen.'

Lyana permits herself a comment as she peels a satsuma. 'Like becoming a thief, wanted by the Green Berets? That trader will report us, Muyu. The boy with the limp. Then they will soon guess that Greenboots is close by.'

'There are many cripples here.'

'True, those who are beaten, who are tortured, rarely stand straight again.

Lyana begins, 'If they catch us –'

The food has restored Muyu's spirits. He beams proudly. 'Let them try!'

Lyana cannot decide whether her friend is growing up or slipping back into boyhood. 'The town is not the forest, Muyu.'

Muyu holds up the portion of grapes reserved for Greenboots. His gaze is distant and all at once fierce, resolved. 'This is how we must take back our island, Lyana.' He shakes the grapes with a cold rage she has never seen in her friend before. 'We seize what is ours!'

For Lieutenant Gani, the debriefing at the central barracks has gone surprisingly smoothly. He has been given the kind of treatment he feels is his due: a meal, a shower, a fresh uniform; and his story has been accepted. The duty officer is thrilled: 'So Greenboots is sailing right into our midst, you say, Lieutenant? A capture indeed! Among many things, he will be charged as an accessory to murder.'

'Then Captain Selim –'

'Died from his wound. Loss of blood. And, er –'

'And, sir?'

'His pride, of course. No man – anyway, Selim is dead and the city is on the alert for his killer.' The officer looks to Gani for confirmation. 'Before he died, Selim accused a young woman. It's obvious, I suppose –'

'Obvious, sir?'

'Doing *that* to a man can only be woman's work, Lieutenant. And this one's got to be a bitch from hell to do it to the Butcher of all people.'

Johannes Gani remembers Lyana with fondness. To confess even a hint of affection for her would be ridiculous. Yet he is not prepared to testify against her. 'I was not a witness, sir.'

'Selim swore it was a girl of the tribe which launched the attack on the timber workers, though I guess it's not as simple as that.'

'From what I can tell, sir – and I don't wish to speak ill of the dead – half the women on the island would've been glad to do the same.'

The commanding officer coughs, stubs out his cigarette. 'The justice of the dagger, eh?' He nods. 'I admire her courage, for the less said about Selim's reputation as a womanizer, the better. Of course he will be buried with full military honours; a hero of the empire.'

Smiles are exchanged. 'And the true story must never come out. The captain had enough life left in him to say that Greenboots was guided from captivity by this same girl and a boy with a limp, son of the chief. Security and the Kopassus are searching the city for them now.'

The officer adds, 'We shall need you for a witness, Lieutenant. You will be able to recognize them?'

Gani is surprised at himself; why is he covering

up for his enemies? 'I'm not sure, sir. The forest people look very much alike.'

'The girl, according to Selim, is a beauty.'

'I really didn't notice, sir.'

'Very well. Now the United Nations delegation will be in session this afternoon at the residency, hearing carefully selected deputations. Tomorrow you will escort them on a tour of some suitably docile villages. They are to see a happy island, do you understand? Happy, united, at peace, content with those who rule over them.'

Gani risks a joke. 'In short, sir, the impossible.'

Fortunately for Gani the officer sees the joke, even appreciates it. 'True. And the day after, when the delegation has taken flight, never to return, the order will be made for repression as usual. In the meantime, enjoy the town. If it's a woman you want –'

'I'd rather, if you don't mind, sir, complete my mission – to bring Greenboots in.'

The officer smiles. 'You – and five thousand Kopassus wanting a crack at him. We have arrested Mueller's friends in town, including Sister Osario. Her famous wooden church regrettably burnt down overnight.

'The place is being watched twenty-four hours a day. And we have a tail on Greenboots' girl-friend, the Aussie journalist, Bryson. She slipped past Security and is now making a nuisance of herself.

'The order from above is that Greenboots does not open his mouth to the delegation.'

*

As Johannes Gani crosses the barrack square
after his debriefing he spots a familiar autocycle, its rider sprawled in the shade and sur-
rounded by his reward for being the eyes and ears
of Security – a six-pack of Pepsi in its new blue
uniform.

Gani has already guessed that Emily Bryson's
'tail' was the boy-spy Benni with an 'i', whom he
met during the first days of his posting to the
island. The duty officer had cautioned Gani about
the boy: 'Do not trust him, Lieutenant. We suspect
the miserable little wretch of being a double agent.
When we find out for sure, we'll rip off his balls
and shoot him. But not before we permit him to
take us to Rosales.'

'He seems very bright, sir. He will already have
guessed we suspect him.'

The officer had shrugged. 'Unless we cut his
throat I guess he'll one day be prime minister of
this island.'

'I think he's more ambitious than that, sir. Nothing less than being president of the empire will
suffice.'

'Then we should certainly have to shoot him!'

Gani pauses, approaches the double spy destined one day to be president. 'Benni, right?'

'You remember me, Lieutenant?'

'Benni with an "i"?'

'Yeah, and you're Johannes with a "j",
right, boss – you want whisky, nice woman,
big tits?'

'No, but I'll swap a bit of advice for a bit of news.'

'What bit?'

'Let's walk.'

'First you give me advice.'

'They think they're on to you, my friend. A double spy.'

Benni cocks his leg over his autocycle. His grin is as wide as the estuary below them. 'That's not worth the big news, boss.'

'Do you have to keep calling me boss?'

'Yes, boss. You boss if you pay me, correct?'

'Don't use that word, please.'

'Captain Selim did – all the time. You got his Ray-bans, boss?'

'Of course not!'

'Poor Butcher in the Shades, eh, boss?'

'I don't want to –'

'Horrible, not having any balls. And no dick!'

'Listen, one more word of that –'

'What's she like, boss, the girl?'

Gani forces himself to be calm. 'You were about to give me some news, Benni.'

'Greenboots is in town!'

Already? 'Which means you know where – tell me!'

'You got my ticket for Jakarta, boss? Five-star hotel, jacussi, dinner on a silver tray – champagne?'

'And what's the price of information about a boy with a limp and a girl with a knife?'

Benni strokes his chin. 'Mm, that will cost you

ten days in Hollywood, boss. And a night with Sharon Stone!'

Perhaps Muyu and Lyana have been talking too loudly, for they have not heard the soft purr of an autocycle as it noses along the narrow track ahead. The bike has stopped. Now they see the rider, a youth, laughing as though he has just got the point of a joke.

'No knives, please!' he says. He puts up his own hands as if to prove his honest intention. 'You looking for some place, maybe – like a house of prayer, church with wooden spire?'

He stays his ground: the boy looks dangerous; and from the stories Benni has heard, the girl *is* dangerous. There is a reward for their capture – enough to send him on a world cruise; or at least a trip to the capital, with breakfast on a silver tray.

'I'm called Benni – with an "i". Friend of Sister Osario.' He waits, ever cheerful. He presses on. 'But going to church, not good idea. Very popular with soldiers at moment.' He sniffs, glances back over his shoulder. 'Also, bad fire. Worshippers pray under sky in future.'

Lyana wonders, why is he speaking to them as if they do not know the language of their own country?

'Me your friend.' Benni waits. He draws a cross over his heart. 'Honest.' Muyu and Lyana permit Benni to roll forward two turns of his autocycle wheels. It's going to be easy: forest folk will believe anything you tell them. 'And you need a friend, correct?'

Lyana begins, 'We can do without being patronized, thank you.'

'"Patronized" – what's that mean?'

Muyu has no intention of allowing a conversation over the meaning of words. With a swiftness which surprises even Lyana, he skips past the rider, drags him off the machine and before Benni with an 'i' can utter another word pins him to the ground with a blade at his throat.

The young spy makes a weak attempt at a struggle, raising his legs as if to lock them around his captor, but Lyana has joined the attack. She jams Benni's legs flat on damp earth.

'My jeans!' It is almost a scream. 'My new Levi's – you've ruined them. Jesus, and I was here to help you!'

Lyana does the interrogating. 'What has happened to Sister Osario – and how do you know we are looking for her?'

All Benni can think about at this moment is the mud soaking through his jeans. He complains bitterly, 'These're special import Levi's. There's only ten other pairs on the island.'

Lyana relaxes, though an inner voice warns her to be careful of this charmer. 'Answer our questions.'

'This isn't mud,' protests Benni, struggling and as he does so splattering his captors. 'It's shit. Horrible. And the damp, it's bringing on my arthritis.'

Muyu is unmoved and unamused: 'Talk!'

Lyana repeats, 'How do you know our business?'

Benni is revising his opinions about forest folk. They are not a pushover after all. 'Okay, what's new? I know everything about everybody. That's *my* business.'

'You're a spy.'

'Hey, not so loud. How else am I going to pay for my education?' He gazes at Lyana. 'You look intelligent, you should try it. Education, I mean. Then you too could get some Levi's.'

The more charming the boy-spy tries to be, the less patient Muyu becomes. He grabs Benni by the ears and the back of his head. He threatens to beat the answer out of him. 'Okay, okay. I surrender. But this is no way to treat a friend of Sister Osario and a fan of Greenboots, not to mention his girlfriend Emily Bryson.'

Muyu repents, loosens his grip. 'Talk!'

Benni is allowed up. He tests the seat of his Levi's with his hand. 'Soaked right through. I'll never get rid of the stain . . . Anyway, I know who you two are. So does every soldier in the city. They're taking bets, who'll bring your heads in.

'The big reward is a posting back home. Think of that, boy with a limp and girl with the dagger! And if you haven't already guessed, your pal Captain Selim is up with the angels. Trying it on with them, no doubt.'

He laughs, glances at Lyana. 'Course, you're

166

Superwoman in the eyes of the people round these parts. Selim shot their sons at Santa Cruz.' His attention turns to Muyu. 'As for you, kid – son of a chief. They'll bang you up, beat you up and hang you out to dry for the sharks.'

The point of Muyu's dagger is perilously close to Benni's throat. 'But me, I'm your friend. I mean, do you or don't you want to meet Sister Osario?'

Muyu turns to Lyana: a nod from her and Benni with an 'i' will be the late Benni with an 'i'. She hesitates; and Benni pounces on the hesitation. 'Make your minds up, folks. Otherwise, I've other business to see to.'

Lyana counts the alternatives open to her and Muyu: they have spared Benni's life. Now they must either trust him or frighten him off. 'Okay, but you walk, not ride. Take us to Sister Osario.'

Benni is still bothered about his jeans. 'I'll consider it. I mean, normally if anybody'd done this to my Levi's I'd report them as Resistance.'

Lyana is stern, unsmiling: she scares Benni. 'Give me the knife, Muyu.'

'Okay, okay – truce. I like my items even better than my Levi's. But what's in this for me?' Benni points at his Levi's. 'Like compensation?'

The silence is cold steel.

Usually nothing can stifle Benni's wit or his brashness but the look in the girl's eyes is clear warning not to underestimate any longer these poor refugees from the forest.

Lyana speaks to the point: 'You want your life?'

He is thinking: Captain Selim didn't stand a chance. 'Yes, please.'

'Then keep your jokes to yourself!'

21

RUNNING OUT OF LUCK

They enter a shanty hut like any other. Its breeze-block walls are unfinished, patched up with asbestos boarding and sheets of bulging plywood. It is windowless except for a gap in the roof which is stuffed with cardboard and straggling balls of old cloth to keep out the rain.

Benni is careful not to leave his machine outside. The handlebar catches against the door lintel. Eyeing the dagger in Lyana's hand, he says, 'You can put that away, miss.'

Lyana gives the order: 'No!' Yet she is willing to help push the autocycle into the black interior.

'All it needs,' Benni is whispering, 'is a bit of trust.'

'Oh yes?'

They wait. Everything is too black to discern whether the room is empty or not. 'Sister Osario? It's me, Benni with an "i". I've brought you some visitors.'

Together, Lyana and Muyu stand perfectly still, counting the moments as their eyes adapt to the gloom. 'They're wanted by the military. And there's a big reward out for them.'

In front of them, sitting behind a table which

takes shape with painful slowness, is a stooped figure.

Something moves. A match is struck. There are hands, a candle and suddenly a glow of light outlines the face of Lieutenant Johannes Gani.

'You!' exclaims Benni with feigned astonishment.

'Me!' Concealed by shade until this moment is a pistol which Gani now points first at Muyu, then at Lyana. 'Welcome to the capital!'

Too stunned to speak or even react, the prisoners simply stare with disbelief. 'Thank you, Benni. Our little strategy worked perfectly.'

'You will need to get them to tell you where Greenboots is hiding,' answers Benni.

'Thank you, my friend. I do not think I need to be reminded of my duties in this matter.'

'Good, then I'll wait outside.'

'First, tie their hands.'

Benni is stubborn and difficult. Tying prisoners' hands behind their backs is not in his contract. 'No rope, sir.'

'Then it is good that I thought ahead. Here.' Gani produces cord. 'Tie them.'

'No good at knots, boss. They always come undone.'

'Do you always talk back to your superiors in this insolent manner?'

Benni grins: 'Always, boss.'

'And I told you not to call me "boss".'

'Sorry, boss.'

Lyana senses that here a game is being played,

and that she and Muyu are part of it. Benni's inso-
lence may appear to be directed at Lieutenant
Gani, but its message also seems to be aimed at
them.

What is he trying to say?

Gani has his speech prepared. 'You must
believe me, but I intend no harm to you two.' He
really means Lyana. 'In fact, I would like to be
your friend.' He is too nervous to inspire fear.
'Really!' He stares past the candlelight at her dim
form. 'And in other circumstances . . .'

Benni has done a poor job with his knots. The
binding is loose; and why, muses Lyana, has he
pressed my hand like that? – as if to say, don't
worry.

'Is it all right to go now, boss?'

Lyana asks Gani, 'What has happened to Sister
Osario?'

'She is under temporary arrest.'

'Boss?'

Gani is tired, stressed, pulled two ways –
between his orders, his duty and his feelings
towards Lyana. It is sheer madness. Turn your
back on her for an instant and she'll slit your
throat (or worse); yet when she stares at me like
this . . .

Benni is permitted to retire. Yet he has been
gone only a moment before he returns. 'Reinforcements, boss.'

'Reinforcements? I didn't –'

Soldiers are entering the room, almost filling
it. Gani stares at them in bewilderment. 'Who

sent you? This is top secret – no need for back-up.'

None of the soldiers speaks. There are eight of them in the room now. Not Gani's regiment, which arrived fresh from Jakarta only weeks before. These are Kopassus, crack troops; the elite; veterans of every major massacre on the island since the invasion.

Even Lieutenant Gani shivers slightly at the sight of them. 'This was unnecessary, gentlemen.' He feels obliged to stand up, come to attention. 'Just a little interrogation of a couple of . . . thieves. See, the fruit – grapes, I think. A minor disciplinary matter.'

Benni pipes up once more. 'Not Kopassus, boss. You can stop sweating.'

'No?'

Benni shrugs as if he too is bewildered. 'Definitely not, boss.'

'Then who are they?'

'It's just a wild guess, boss, but – begging your pardon – I reckon they're pretending.'

'Pretending?' If Johannes Gani had felt the temptation before to shake in the presence of members of Kopassus, he now gives in to that temptation. 'Not . . .'

'Yes, boss – Resistance. Sorry.'

'But –'

'Good disguise, correct?'

The door opens once more. A thin, bearded man, in the uniform of a major, enters. Instead of a military hat he wears a green cricketer's cap complete with the badge of the Australian cricket team.

Gani drops back on to his chair. He has never met this man, but he recognizes him as the acting head of the island's resistance movement: the most hunted man in the whole of the Indonesian empire – Enrico Rosales. He glares at Benni.

'Nothing to do with me, boss.'

There is one more surprise for Johannes Gani as his eyes pass from face to face. 'And you too . . .' He recognizes old friends – Arbi and Teguh, the guards from the timber camp.

They address him in unison: 'Good morning, Lieutenant!'

One of Rosales' men has circled behind Gani, presses a sub-machine-gun into his back. In a light, clipped voice, full of authority, Rosales asks Lyana, 'Has this man done you harm?'

Muyu answers: 'He killed Muyu Father.'

'No!' This voice is Lyana's.

'Has he treated you with any kindness whatever?'

Muyu: 'He followed us. Shot at us. He left us to drown.'

Rosales' gaze rests on Lyana. 'Doing his duty?'

'Yes.' Why is she speaking for this man? Perhaps because of his quiet, sad words; perhaps because she has seen something beyond the pride and bluster – something that deserved another chance.

Rosales asks Benni, 'What was his intention with these two?'

'He fancies the girl, I think.'

'But would he have taken them into detention?'

Benni glances from Muyu to Lyana to Johannes Gani. He knows that a life is in his hands. 'Maybe not.'

'Very well.' Rosales turns to Gani. 'Fortunately for you, Lieutenant, you can be useful to us. At two o'clock this afternoon the United Nations delegation will be hearing evidence of the atrocities committed on this island by your government and its butchers.

'They will learn of the massacres in the forest and the terror our people have been subjected to over the years. You will be of assistance to us in this enterprise.'

'I will not testify!'

Rosales nods. 'Agreed. In fact you will not open your mouth.'

'Then how can I be useful to you?'

'You will escort Enrico Rosales and Hans Mueller, known as Greenboots, to the residency where we will all have tea and crab sandwiches with the delegation.'

'I am an officer of the Indonesian army.'

'Exactly. You are perfect for the job. And you will have these members of Kopassus beside you all the way.' Rosales smiles; but his expression does not conceal a mood which signals to Gani – obey or die. 'For once in your life, Lieutenant, you will be on the side of the angels!'

'I'm no traitor!' yells Gani.

'Of course you are,' is the chilling response.

Rosales points at Gani's former prisoners, the son of a chief and the executioner of his commanding officer. 'You permitted these two to live. For that, you would be court-martialled.'

'So be it, then. I'm sick of the whole business.'

Enrico Rosales shakes his head. 'You are Kopassus. You will escort your prisoners to the residency, and you may yet fill the heart of your father, the general, with pride.

'Now move!'

22

GREENBOOTS' ISLAND

'You wish meet Greenboots, Miss Emily?'

'Not you again – go away. I've had it up to here with spies.'

'Then you not wish see Greenboots?'

Emily Bryson halts. Her way lies back to the governor's residency overlooking the harbour. In under an hour, the United Nations delegation will begin to hear evidence.

'Not my fault Sister Osario arrested, Miss Emily.'

'And don't call me "Miss Emily". It's ridiculous.'

Benni repeats his question, this time more urgently; and then he adds, 'Because if you don't, you better forget him. He need you.'

She stops. Who else is there to trust? 'Where is he?'

'We take ride.'

'I'm not getting on that thing.'

'You got whisky?'

'I got whisky.'

'He need it bad.'

She changes her mind about the ride. 'Okay, but no speeding. This is a built-up area.'

*

Hans Mueller dreams of delivering his testimony. The World Court hangs on his every word. In front of him, in the dock, accused of crimes against the defenceless people of the island, are presidents and prime ministers.

Shame on you all. You armed these killers. You sent planes and guns and bombs and mines. Your helicopters blacken the sky over this island. See the dead – see the crosses on the hills, in the valleys, on Soul Mountain itself. They are the crosses of women and children.

Your work, gentlemen. With your Skyhawks, your F-5 jets, your Broncos, your Hercules transport aircraft, your Alouettes and your Pumas, not to mention your chemical defoliants.

The prime minister of Britain protests: 'Our arms industry promised me the weapons were intended only for peaceful purposes.' He sits down, satisfied. 'Put that in your pipe, Greenboots, and smoke it!'

The president of the United States himself has got to his feet. 'It is totally and absolutely and indubitably untrue to say, as you did in your last book, Greenboots, that this great nation of America which loves freedom above all things would consider the supply of oil to be more important than the lives of the island people.'

'Silence in court!' shouts Greenboots. 'Have you forgotten, Mister President, that the day after one of your predecessors visited this island, the invasion began?'

'We knew nothing! The CIA were on vacation in

Bali. And anyway in 1975 things were different.'

'Oh yes, my friend, when half the population of a country is massacred, there has got to be a difference.'

The Pope wishes to know why he has been summoned to court. 'I'm needed to conduct High Mass in St Peter's, Monsignor Greenboots.'

Hans reminds the Pope of his own visit to the island. 'The Indonesians laughed at you though you never realized it. Did you ever find out that Taci-Toki, where you were permitted an open-air Mass beneath the portrait of the president, father of the island's terror, has been the scene of one of the worst massacres?

'I kissed the earth.'

'It was soaked in blood – read my book!'

The prime minister of Australia has been edging towards the door of the courtroom only to be summoned back by Greenboots who miraculously has had his spectacles restored to him. 'Don't you skulk away, Mister Ozzie-Two-Faces. You more than the rest of these gangsters should hang your head in mortal shame.'

The Aussie prime minister bluffs it out. 'Never touched the ball, umpire. It was off my pad. Truth is, it's just another conspiracy against my boys, like bodyline bowling. I blame the Brits, the Japs, the Portuguese, the Dutch, in no particular order. And I've got three spare tickets for the Adelaide test – any takers?'

The British prime minister seizes them all. 'How-zat!' he shouts.

The courtroom fades as presidents and prime minister fight over the free tickets to the Adelaide test; and Hans Mueller slowly returns to the reality of his other island.

His dream, however, is not quite over. His eyes are open to another vision, of Muyu and Lyana around the night fire in the forest, the wind whispering above them. Greenboots has added the final words to his log of the forest folk. 'Lyana, I want you to keep it, in case anything happens to me.'

The firelight flickers on her face, the high forehead, the arched brows, the mouth that can be gentle and sometimes cruel. 'And what shall I do with it, Hans, without you?'

'I have taught you all I know. All I've read of the world, all I've seen beyond the confines of Mother Forest, I've shared with you. Now it is time for my little bird to open her own wings.'

'And Muyu?'

'Your paths will separate and then one day perhaps come once more together. You, Lyana . . . The opportunities of the world tug at your elbow. Someone must speak as someone must act – you understand me?'

'I have killed a man.'

'Then let the sky alone be your witness – go!'

The river is lapping at Hans Mueller's feet. Soon, if the rains continue, this sanctuary will be washed away. He heaves himself closer to the water. He is feeling much worse. The life is seeping out of him. He is dry but he has not the strength to drink.

Forgetting that the river is the cemetery of rats, he splashes his face with a scoop of water.

I cannot feel my legs. Who needs 'em? Greenboots' island seems to him to begin floating down river. The shore is a yellow blur. This could be the ocean itself, and is that the isle of Atauro astern, where the concentration camps are located?

I believe leprosy is back.

The sun is almost overhead. Hans blinks, shades his half-blind eyes. He hears the strong ripple of water: is that a boat engine? He lifts himself up on to his elbow.

'Lyana – Muyu?'

They're back, his rescuers. The best kids in the world. He fights to get up, raises a hand in joy. He waits. They do not call his name; and at his own words – 'Did you find our missionary?' – there is a silence that fills him with terror.

'Is that you?'

The hopes of Greenboots crash like the forest trees demolished by the Yellow Giants.

Soldiers!

23

FUNERAL MARCH

'We were too late.' These are all the words Enrico
Rosales permits in explanation. His men have
brought in Greenboots on a stretcher. There is a
groundsheet over his body and over his face. Only
his Doc Martens show, drooping over the end of
the stretcher.

'It is time. On your feet, Lieutenant Gani: this
is to be your hour of glory.'

Lyana feels Muyu's arm comfortingly around
her. This is not Muyu. It cannot be true. Greenboots
was injured; he was ill. But his long sleep, and
the whisky – they seemed to have restored his
body as well as his spirits.

Greenboots, dead: impossible, but here lies the
evidence.

Gani also stares at the body on the stretcher. 'I
did not want this to happen. It is nothing to do
with me.'

Rosales' men take up the stretcher. Lyana steps
forward. Her hand is stretched out to take hold
of the corner of the groundsheet which covers
Greenboots.

'No time!'

Rosales makes Gani's task clear. 'You will escort
your prisoners and the body of this dead hero to

the residency. They are your prize, Lieutenant, for which you will gain esteem, praise – medals, even. But be warned. Try betraying us and the first bullet in this gun is reserved for you.'

'We'll be seen!' protests Gani, still unable to grasp his part in Rosales' plans.

'Exactly: we march straight through the town.'

'And if we're stopped?'

'We are Kopassus, remember. Nobody dares stop Kopassus.'

'And afterwards?'

'You continue to do what I tell you.'

This time Benni has obeyed orders. He has retied Muyu's and Lyana's hands; effectively but not so tightly that the cord hurts; and he has chosen to bind their hands at the front rather than behind their backs.

'Sorry.'

Lyana is too sad to speak. She loves Greenboots as much as she reveres him. Because of him, she reads; her knowledge has opened beyond the limits of the forest and the island. He has fed her visions of what might be, of what a future built on liberty might hold.

And Muyu, he too has been the disciple of Greenboots, though for him what he will miss most are Greenboots' stories told around the night fires, of heroes of faraway lands.

Tonight, Thor, God of Thunder.

Tonight, Odysseus on his long voyage home.

Tonight, William Tell who shot the apple from his son's head.

Tonight, Robin Hood who roamed his very own Mother Forest and fought for the rights of his people.

'And one day, who knows? Perhaps they will talk of Muyu the Brave who slew the Yellow Giants.'

There are tears in Lyana's eyes. Things have been bad, yet never until this moment, as the body of Hans Mueller, the beloved Greenboots, is carried before her, has she been without hope.

However dark the present, there has always been the reassuring thought – Greenboots will know what to do. Greenboots possesses the treasure of knowledge from which he draws the lessons of the past, and which guides his vision of the future.

This is your time of leaving, Lyana – you in particular, for you have the gift; you have the openness of mind. The forest cannot contain you for ever.

I would be unhappy away from the forest.

Yes, maybe. But Mother Forest is patient. She will await your return, as the world awaits you now.

I do not understand.

You will.

And my destiny, Greenboots?

To talk for your people.

Me?

Yes.

But I have not your words.

You can learn them.

*

It is left for Benni to remind Lyana of her precious cargo. 'You want me to carry that?' He points to her rucksack, still clinging to her shoulders like a scared monkey.

She has lost Greenboots, but his log is safe. She says, 'No!'

The boy-spy seems to understand. 'Then good luck, my lady of the dagger!'

They are out, away from the narrow alleys of shanty town. Lyana looks about her for the first time. The story of Greenboots' capture has spread throughout the capital. As if forewarned – which they might have been by the Resistance – crowds line the route; and in mourning.

The mighty Greenboots is dead; the little man with the big words, who spoke up for the tribes; put this beleaguered island on the world map with his writings and his films and his broadcasts – made the Distant Masters smart with rage.

Shot through the heart by Kopassus.

With Hans Mueller gone, truly this will be the Island of the Empty Huts. Somehow Greenboots' death has sharpened the vision of him, enlarged it, projected it upon the consciousness of the people as if on a giant screen.

After its initial silence, the crowd – as the procession passes – gently then forcefully begins to hiss. Then the hiss assumes another shape, the opening of a word:

'Sha . . .'

The word is a sentiment, a belief, a power; and it grows:

'Shananaa . . . Shananaa!'

There are soldiers in the crowd. They grasp well enough the message in the word.

'Shananaa!' It is defiant; its meaning is resistance. The soldiers shoot into the air as a warning, but unless they kill everyone in the crowd there is no stopping the hissing; and in their ears the sound resembles a bomb about to explode:

'Shananaa . . . Shananaa!'

'What are they saying, Benni?' asked Gani, remembering the sound from the time he had gone to receive his orders from Colonel Fario.

'You not know, Lieutenant?'

'No, I not know – tell me!'

Benni raises one arm to the crowd as if conducting them. 'They're saying "Shananaa", boss.'

'But what does it mean?'

'You're a spy like me, aren't you? But pretty useless, I'd say.'

The crowd wonders who these forest folk are, hands tied, walking behind the stretcher, heads bowed.

The young chief who led the rebellion?

And the girl – isn't she beautiful? – but oh how sad; the one who they say took her revenge on the officer they call the Butcher.

He shot my boy before my eyes.

He took my brothers.

Remember Santa Cruz.

He was a monster. She did what we'd all do, given the chance.

And the courage.

'Bless you, child!'

They'll be topped.

Tortured first.

And look at the cat with the cream – that lieutenant shot Greenboots and brought in those kids.

They'll be rolling out the red carpet for him in Jakarta, Hell take him!

Despite the number of soldiers and security men in the crowd, none dares note a resemblance – between this Kopassus officer, the one wearing the Australian cricket cap, and the face on posters all over town of the island's most wanted man, Enrico Rosales.

The world is blind when Kopassus rules.

The funeral procession approaches the formidable barbed wire fences surrounding the residency. The gates open, guards salute. One spits at the body of Greenboots.

'Let's 'ave 'is DMs, Lieutenant,' calls one soldier. 'He'll not be needin' 'em any more.'

Lieutenant Gani looks into space. He hears nothing, says nothing. To himself, he says, 'That's right – hail the conquering hero ... Marching straight to his death.'

Beside him, his autocycle coughing up its usual stream of blue exhaust, is Benni. He refuses to 'Beat it!' as Gani commands him to.

He is grinning. 'Don't worry, boss. Who knows, this could be your lucky day after all!'

24

REVELATIONS

So far, grief at the loss of Greenboots has numbed Lyana. She has felt no fear, only a kind of dizziness, as if nothing of this is really happening. Having passed through luxurious gardens, they are mounting the residency steps.

In all this there has been one good thing, the call of the crowd, their support. To whisper the magic word 'Shananaa...' is to invite arrest, mutilation and murder. Yet under the gaze of the military the island people have communicated their resolve and defied their masters.

Her eyes are on the body of her friend beneath the groundsheet. As the stretcher is tilted by Rosales' men, the right arm of the corpse slips from its cover. It dangles in space as the Resistance carry the stretcher into an imposing reception hall.

Each step increases Lyana's sense of terror, for though the trap door is open now, though this daring and arrogant strategy of Rosales appears to be succeeding, Security will surely have become suspicious.

Our luck can't hold.

Yet there is another emotion – curiosity – struggling for attention in her brain, aroused by that sudden glimpse of Greenboots' arm. For a few seconds, unnoticed by Rosales and his men, the arm had swayed loose.

They have now thrust it back in place beside the body; covered it once more with the dark green shroud.

Lyana feels the blood pounding through her head. She almost cries out, checks her stride. The dizziness is something else, more powerful yet bringing to her thoughts only confusion:

Greenboots never had a tattoo.

She looks at Muyu, would like to speak, but they are climbing marble steps. Great windows ahead cast a brilliant light along balustrades and down the stairwell.

This is not Greenboots. She is breathless as if she had climbed to the summit of the high forest.

Beyond the steep rear gardens planted with orange trees and tall flowering shrubs is the ocean; and far out – black humps and peaks with trailing tails – are the outer islands.

Largest and nearest is Atauro island where Lyana's cousin was taken, never to return. Rosales is speaking to the guards at the top of the stairs. He dismisses them. 'From now on, Kopassus guard the delegation.'

To Muyu Lyana whispers, 'That isn't Greenboots!'

Muyu touches her affectionately, reassuringly with the back of his tied hands. His face is running with tears. 'Those are his boots, Lyana. For certain.'

The United Nations observers are seated at the

office desk of Colonel Fario. Four of them. The chairperson is a senator from Pennsylvania in America. She has introduced herself to the press and photographers.

Like her colleagues, Mrs Betty O'Farrell has been suffering from the heat, though this irritates her less than Mr Hindarto, the governor's press officer, who seems to be under orders never to let her out of his sight.

Her first question to Hindarto had concerned Emily Bryson.

'Not present, madam.'

'She spoke to me this morning on the telephone. I assured her of a safe conduct.'

'Not present, madam.'

'Then where is she?'

'She went to the city.'

'She was followed?'

'For her own safety, madam. The Resistance, you see – very dangerous.'

'The authorities claim that there is no Resistance.'

'We mop up last few, Senator.'

'Then I want you to send out a search party for Miss Bryson. She will be particularly grief-stricken at the news of the death of Greenboots.'

'Greenboots, madam?'

'You know who I mean, Mr Hinderito.'

'Hindarto, madam. And I think you refer to the German national, Herr Mueller, who was an illegal immigrant. A criminal who had much blood on his hands.'

The inquiry room door is held wide open. There is hesitation as to who should enter first – Lieutenant Gani or Rosales.

'You!' commands Rosales. Gani obeys, clicks his heels, salutes the delegation. He has no alternative: there is a gun at his back.

He thinks, This is a fiasco but I'll carry it through.

'We can do without all these soldiers,' says Senator O'Farrell. 'This is a human rights commission, not a court-martial.'

Rosales ignores her. His twelve men follow the stretcher which is laid on the polished floor in front of the delegation.

Two of Rosales' men – Arbi and Teguh, enjoying life as usual – return through the door, stand guard on the other side.

'I said, we have no requirements for military protection . . . Mr Hindrita?'

It is not only the civilians of the town, or the forest folk, who are terrified by the presence of Kopassus. Mr Hindarto is trembling, and silent; yet not because he is all at once close to men who would slaughter the entire population of a village if any should so much as question their actions, but because he has recognized Enrico Rosales.

He has also recognized Lieutenant Johannes Gani, the secret agent sent to the forest to 'make Greenboots disappear'. Hindarto decides he must excuse himself immediately, warn Colonel Fario.

This is a trick; and a disgraceful lapse in secur-
'If you will excuse me for a moment, madam.'

If all of these people were to be arrested before they left the residency, just for once in his life Mr Hindarto might be praised rather than blamed. He bows, steps towards the rear door.

'Stay where you are!' Rosales' push is not so violent that it would throw Hindarto off balance; but it is on the floor that Hindarto prefers to be.

They are going to kill everyone!

Rosales has removed his green cricket cap. He introduces himself. 'You can see, Senator, the measures one has to take to exercise freedom of speech in this island.'

Mrs O'Farrell is impressed but disapproving. 'We can hardly be expected to give a hearing to the so-called leader of a resistance movement that does not exist.'

'First, Senator, I am merely the deputy leader of this movement, for you know full well that our leader, our president, is rotting in Jakarta's Cipiang prison at this moment.'

Now at last Johannes Gani recognizes what the crowd has been whispering: Shananaa . . . Xanana, the people's warrior, ambushed by the military after the biggest manhunt in the history of the empire.

XANANA IS CAPTURED. How the press in Jakarta had celebrated.

Senator O'Farrell convinces no one, not even herself, with her reply to Rosales. 'We are doing everything in our power to win an amnesty for your leader.'

'He will crap on your amnesty, Senator. Only

when this island is set at liberty will Xanana Gusmao talk peace with Bapaks. Till then, in the words of our leader, Gusmao – We resist to win!'

An observer from Australia, like his government anxious not to upset the Indonesian regime with too much criticism, butts in. 'The authorities in Jakarta have worked impressively to improve the human rights record here and on the other islands. We have had personal assurances from the president himself. Talking is what must take place, not fighting.'

The silence is as cold as midnight in the forest. The photographers forget to press the shutters of their cameras. The only sound is of the unoiled fan on the ceiling trundling in vain to disperse the combination of nature's hot air with that made by humans.

Rosales advances a step towards the table. The Australian sits back as if he fears being struck. 'Tomorrow, Senator and gentlemen, as you take plane for your homeland, content to accept the lies that say things on the island are improving, ten thousand troops will use their bayonets to prove who's boss.'

'We have assurances!' responds the Australian hotly.

Senator O'Farrell dries her forehead. She is confused. She has so little information; even less understanding. 'I earnestly hope there will not be reprisals, Mr Hinditero.'

'Hindarto, madam. I am afraid I know nothing of this.'

'I suspect you know everything!'

'It is a military matter.'

The room is crackling once more with flash-photos. Reporters are clustering round, sticking microphones first in Rosales' direction, then towards Hindarto and finally Senator O'Farrell.

Rosales calms things by waving his Kalashnikov at the reporters. 'You'll get your facts.' He turns to Senator O'Farrell. 'It is very likely we shall have to shoot our way out of this building.' He points to Lyana and Muyu. 'I would ask that these two young people are taken into your protection. They are the friends of Greenboots here. They are wanted by the authorities.'

Rosales now nods at the stretcher bearers. As he speaks, his eyes are on Lyana and Muyu. 'Remove the cover.'

Lyana sees before anything else the right arm bearing a tattoo, of a serpent coiled around initials. The body of a stranger lies before her and her relief is immense; for she had begun to doubt her memory, wondering whether Greenboots really had a tattoo, one he had perhaps kept hidden.

Lyana's heart has been borne down by a sadness as vast as Soul Mountain; yet her relief is mixed with fear – is Greenboots still alone and helpless on the island?

The storms are coming: they will wash him away into the ocean.

Rosales is saying, staring gravely down at the corpse, 'This is Hans Mueller, madam. Killed in a senseless and brutal raid upon the forest village of these two young people.' His steely expression relaxes as he glances towards Lyana and Muyu. 'These are the sole survivors of one of the most ancient tribes in the world. It was genocide!

'Now that Mueller, known to the island people as Greenboots, cannot testify for himself, I wish these young people to speak for him, and for themselves.'

The body stinks. Senator O'Farrell rams a handful of tissues under her nose. 'Anything, so long as you . . . remove the corpse.'

Rosales' speech is not complete. Once more he indicates Lyana and Muyu. 'These young people, Senator, are the most precious treasure of any society – they are its future. This island ultimately belongs to them. They are its destiny.'

Lyana has watched Johannes Gani's face. He too has gasped, with shock, and then with relief, at the body of the stranger with the tattoo. He is staring back at her, almost smiling; wanting somehow to share with her this moment in which – so it would seem – the shadow of the assassin has been lifted from him.

Neither Senator O'Farrell and the other United Nations observers nor the press are to be let into the secret of the true identity of the dead man. Portraits of hero Greenboots, with famous green DMs – and that unmistakable serpent tattoo on his right arm – will be on the front pages of the world's press by the weekend.

Lyana and Muyu are invited to give evidence

of the massacre carried out in the high forest by Captain Selim and his men. And they tell more, of villages destroyed, their people buried in pits and covered with lime; of men and women lined up and shot; of victims taken up in planes and helicopters and thrown out into the sky.

Lyana's own parents could read and write. For that reason and that reason alone, they were taken out of their village, shot and left in a ditch.

'That is all in the past,' protests the Australian.

Lyana stares him out. 'It is now, sir. And it is everywhere.'

'They've opened schools.'

'They do not permit us to speak our own language.'

'They've spent thousands of dollars –'

'To teach us how to be good Indonesians.'

'What's wrong with that?'

'We are not Indonesians!'

There is a knock at the door. Arbi enters. He whispers to his chief. Rosales signals to his men. 'I am afraid, Senator, we shall have to take our leave. We have been found out. We shall make our exit by the rear gardens.'

'And Greenboots?'

'We consign his body to your safekeeping.'

Rosales has one more task to complete. 'Muyu?' He nods towards the corpse. 'Take the boots. They're yours. Do as I say!'

He addresses the reporters and photographers in a blaze of flashlights. 'Gentlemen, tomorrow the Indonesian press will trumpet the news that

Enrico Rosales was killed while attempting to murder the United Nations delegation.

'You are witnesses that I came and went in peace ... What you can be sure of is that this delegation will be prevented from continuing its inquiries. They will be flown out on the next plane to ensure their safety. And you – the eyes and ears of the world – will be on board with them.'

The reporter who spoke up before asks, 'If we get a chance to talk to Xanana in Cipiang jail, what's your message?'

'Tell him – *un grande abraco* – a hug from all his comrades. And all his people!'

25

WHERE THE LAND MEETS THE SEA

For Lyana in these moments, hope has slid back into despair. True, the discovery that Greenboots might still be alive has filled her with a strange new joy. Yet all the signs are bad ones.

When Rosales' men went with Muyu to Greenboots' island in the river they must have not found him. Had he wandered; been taken or fallen into the water and drowned?

Is he at this moment crying out under the hand of the torturer or submerged somewhere along the river amidst stinking refuse, awaiting the hunger of rats in the night?

Yet where had Hans' green DMs come from?

There is no more time to consider such mysteries. Rosales' men have thrown open the French windows on to a veranda. The residency is beginning to echo with distant shouts, drawing nearer. A gun is fired, then another.

Simultaneously alarms sound all over the city; and in the residency itself every corridor and room is flashing with red lights in accompaniment to the deafening scream of sirens.

Muyu acts on his instinct alone. There is no protection these people behind the polished desk can offer him which is worth a fallen leaf. He has Lyana by the hand, pulling her.

They came with the Resistance fighters; they will leave with them.

'Come!'

She obeys, her fears at one with his. Out now, down the balcony steps. Rosales and his men spray the gardens ahead with gunfire. All at once, running, Lyana glances back. She sees, framed in the wide shade of the French window, Johannes Gani, forlorn, half in the residency, half out, half staying, half following.

She halts, calls, answering her own instinct. She beckons; and Gani wrenches himself from an old life, leaping steps, eyes wide yet dazed, mind both tormented and wild with the thrill of the choice he has made.

Troops of the real Kopassus are on the residency roof, firing. Their shots hit marble urns, splinter stone, ricochet. Teguh falls, rises again, a bullet through his leg. His friend Arbi returns for him.

'Leave me!'

'Don't be such a nerd!' Arbi scoops Teguh on to his shoulder.

Close-cropped lawns dip steeply past ornamental pools. A cupid aiming his bow across shimmering water towards a reclining Venus is hit and decapitated. Bullets shatter the roof of a miniature pagoda. One passes so close to Muyu and Lyana that as they run they hear the wind and whistle of it.

Residency guards, backed by Kopassus, are

racing round the house, pouring from the French windows, ignoring the United Nations delegation. Senator O'Farrell has been thrust out of the way. The Australian has been ordered to raise his hands; the press corps is herded into a corner of the room.

'No photographs!'

In their panic, Security seem to have quite forgotten they are dealing with a United Nations delegation which has been guaranteed its safety on the island. They are prisoners. They talk with rebels, and that is enough to justify forcing them to lie on their faces.

Doubtless they are part of a world conspiracy to support the rebels. Even so, two photographers have broken away from their huddle. The room flashes with camera light. Mr Hindarto alone rescues them from being shot.

'It is all a mistake.' His voice is drowned by gunfire, though Senator Betty O'Farrell, sprawled on her chest, with a soldier's boot in her back, hears it well enough.

All at once she has begun to share the terror the island population has experienced ever since the Indonesians followed invasion with the butchery of occupation. 'Mr Hindarto, my president will hear of this!'

'I assure you, madam, things will soon be back to normal. The Resistance will be exterminated.'

Indeed for Rosales' men, for Lyana, Muyu and Johannes Gani, the pursuit is desperate: what had appeared an escape route through the residency gardens has terminated in space.

The gardens not only overlook the sea; they stop at the sea. This is where the island ends and the ocean begins. The entire length of this part of the residency meets a single boundary; indeed the prime element of the residency's security.

There is a tiled path, a waist-high balustrade, and after that – nothing. The cliff face falls sheer to the sea. And the cliff face is as smooth as ivory: a wall of reinforced concrete.

'Anyone for a swim?' Rosales is there ahead of his men. Talking almost to himself, striving to be as casual as possible, he says of the perilous drop below them, 'It means getting wet, of course.'

Arbi is panting under the weight of Teguh. He stares over the edge of the precipice and grunts. 'If we get separated, Teguh, we'll meet at the bottom, okay?'

Teguh sees nothing as he is facing back towards the residency. 'It's your call, pal!'

Mr Hindarto has managed to restore Senator O'Farrell to her feet. He attempts to brush her down.

'Don't touch me, you horrible little man.'

Unruffled, he points out of the French windows. 'In a few moments, Senator, peace will be restored, I assure you. Look, our enemies face the tallest cliff on the island. They must surrender to Kopassus or fall to their deaths.'

*

Rosales gazes at Lyana and Muyu; points a finger which is both reproving and admiring. 'It was your choice. You still have a chance to go back. No?'

Lyana shakes her head.

Rosales glances at the former Lieutenant Gani. For an instant Lyana fears that he is going to shoot Johannes. Instead Rosales peers over the balustrade. 'Somewhere out there, we have a boat waiting. I only hope no one has a bad head for heights.'

Johannes Gani finds himself to be weirdly calm. 'What the hell?' He holds out his hands, to Lyana and to Muyu. 'My apologies.'

Together they climb the final balustrade – Johannes, Lyana, Muyu, Rosales and his men. Arbi is levering Teguh into a space peppered with bullets.

From the top of the hill a machine-gun takes off the heads of pine trees which have dared block its aim.

Rosales raises his arms and yells, and as he does so his comrades tune in to his ringing declaration: '*Viva* Timor Leste – Long Live East Timor!'

The sky and the wind and the sea seem to unite in a chorus of approval. 'Shananaa!' they reply.

EPILOGUE

Surprise parcel

'Who do you know in Portugal?'

He has been staring out from this tiny apartment balcony past the botanical gardens, away across Farm Cove towards Sydney's magnificent Harbour Bridge. Only today has he felt the strength and the motivation to open Emily Bryson's laptop computer. He has typed no more than a title – JUSTICE OF THE DAGGER. He has everything to do again.

At least he's got new spectacles.

Emily places a parcel on the table in front of Hans Mueller. 'Postmark Lisbon.'

Hans, once the Bearded One, once Greenboots and now Emily Bryson's sickly lodger, has suffered recurring fever since the island Resistance rescued him. Under cover of darkness he had been ferried from island to island until he could join a ship for Australia.

Since then he has been restless and depressed. He has had no news of his friends: no message from the Resistance; and he mourns – for Muyu, Lyana and his forest life.

He is also depressed because he has lost his precious log, containing, so he had recounted to his Australian friends, 'the story of a people whose simple life, of community and sharing, are an example to us all. I loved them!'

Yet Greenboots' mood is about to change. He unwraps the parcel. 'Emily!' He lets go a cry of exultation which almost halts the traffic on Sydney Bridge. 'A miracle!'

'They've found your DMs?'

He holds out to her the half-unwrapped parcel containing the plastic-bound pages of his log, scarcely one page missing or damaged. 'It's all here!'

Emily Bryson celebrates the instant change in her lover. 'Is there a letter?'

He fumbles, allows Emily to take the log. 'Got to be!'

She finds a blue envelope, unfolds it for him.

'You read it.'

'It's signed "Lyana"!'

'From Lisbon? . . . Read it, Em.'

'She's gone there to study.'

'Just what I said she must do!'

'Hang on, my Portuguese isn't wonderful . . . Who was Johannes?'

'The only Johannes I knew was – heavens, don't say he decided to join the side of the angels?'

'Looks like it.'

'I knew there was a bond growing between those two. A love of opposites, eh?'

'Johannes sends you a message, Greenboots – of friendship.'

'Well, that only backs my instinct about him. A

convert, that's what he was. You'll see, the two of them will return ... They'll be unstoppable. The future will have to be struggled for, but – mark my words – it will belong to them!'

Emily smiles. Her relief is profound: Greenboots lives! – back to form in both hope and vanity.

'And what news is there of Muyu, Emily? By my reckoning he'd never leave the island.'

'Correct again, Professor ... Lyana writes that Muyu returned to the forest.'

'With the Resistance? Of course! So Muyu fights on.' Hans Mueller shuts his eyes, dreams. Sydney Harbour Bridge vanishes in a mist rising from the forest. 'Muyu!'

On a rock escarpment shielded by trees, and over-looking a valley so steep even the midday sun scarcely touches it, shadows move against the light. Enrico Rosales, commander of the Resistance in the absence of his leader, Xanana, imprisoned in Jakarta, is accompanied by his forest guide.

Thanks to Muyu, the Resistance have, in Enrico's words, 'run the army ragged'.

The latest campaign to rid the island of opposition to Indonesian rule is at this moment lost in the blind-dark valley. As the Bapak troops climb up into the light, dazzled by the sudden opening of the sky, they will meet men whose homes they have destroyed; whose families they have turned into forest cemeteries.

This morning the forest clearances stopped. The sound of trees crashing into undergrowth gave way to the silence which Muyu's people had cherished since the beginning of time. In another ravine almost locked away from the sun, there is one more cemetery – though the dead have been too large and too cumbersome to bury: the Yellow Giants have taken a great fall.

Their keeper, a man called Marquez, has grumbled a bit. But his curse has been mainly for the forest, for its tangle and its heat and the things that sting and bite.

He has gone back to the capital with stories of another Greenboots. 'Saw him in the forest. He's got a bad limp, but you couldn't miss those DMs. I reckon it's the chief's son. One day that kid will be calling the shots around these parts.'

Another shadow on the hill is getting used to walking instead of riding an autocycle; but Benni with an 'i' has every intention of returning soon to spread more mischief among his military employers.

'Greenboots has returned from the dead!' Benni will add to the tales set off by Marquez; and as the tales circulate they will grow strong in the telling. The people will recognize the urges which bind them – the desire for liberty, for the right to tell their own stories in their own language and in their own way.

'Greenboots lives!'

For the present this news from the forest will give the people the courage to turn their whispers of protest into a great shout. On the forest wind, the chant carries across the island, across the ocean.

Lyana also dreams. One day, when she has completed her studies here in the country that once conquered and ruled her people, she will return with Johannes to her island of the empty huts; and to her friend Muyu.

Mother Forest whispers her own eventual welcome, imitating, as if in sympathy and love, the murmur of the island's people:

'Shananaa!'

Author's Note

Before first light on Monday 26 January 1996 a break-in occurred at the British Aerospace factory test site at Warton, Lancashire. Damage estimated at £2 million was found to have been caused to a Hawk jet destined for Indonesia. With hammers, the intruders had disabled those features of the plane connected to weaponry – the nose cone, radar, bomb attachment under the wings and control devices in the cockpit.

The action was not that of the IRA, the KGB, Arab terrorists or mindless vandals on a spree. It was the work of women protestors who, having committed their offence, made no attempt to escape. Instead, they phoned the press and waited for Security to come and arrest them. Andrea Needham, Joanna Wilson, Lotta Kronlid and Angie Zelter were imprisoned and charges of conspiracy and criminal damage laid against them.

The motive for this seemingly wilful destruction is signalled by what the women left with the Hawk fighter plane – banners, seeds and ashes. Planted on this engine of death were photographs of the children of victims of a brutal massacre by the Indonesian troops, on 12 November 1991, at the church of Santa Cruz on the island of East

Timor. The seeds represented a campaign entitled 'Seeds of Hope' whose supporters argue that weapons must be turned to ploughshares. The demolition of the Hawk was a symbolic act; a fervent protest that such weapons must not be exported for use by nations to suppress their own peoples.

Justice of the Dagger is neither a history nor a documentary. It is a work of fiction, a creation. Yet when readers recall references to Hawk aircraft, or the slaughter of civilians – mainly students – at Santa Cruz, I hope they will spare a thought for those, like the intruders at Warton, who risk their own freedom in order to support the rights of others to be free from repression.

At Liverpool Crown Court in July 1996 the defendants pleaded Not Guilty, arguing that their actions at Warton had been in a 'higher cause': they were using reasonable force to prevent a crime, forestalling the military use to which the Hawk ZH955 might be put by the Indonesian military.

To everyone's amazement, but to the joy of all those who saw both justice and courage in the actions of the 'ploughshares' women, the jury cleared the accused of the charges against them. That was a golden letter day in the struggle for human rights. This did not, of course, prevent British Aerospace serving a civil injunction on the women who, to cheers, promptly tore it up outside the court.

It was shortly after the court decision in Liverpool that the Indonesian people themselves took to the streets of Jakarta in protest at the repressive rule of President Suharto.

In October 1996 there was to be another golden letter day: the Nobel Prize for Peace was awarded to East Timor's bishop, Carlos Belo, and to exiled resistance leader, José Ramos-Horta, for their 'sustained and self-sacrificing contributions for a small but oppressed people'. Bishop Belo, taking Mass in the island's capital when the award was announced, declared that the prize 'represents the very hard work we still have to do'.

If this moment represented a glimpse of light through dark clouds, it was not to signal an end to the anguish of East Timor. In the autumn of 1997 a horrible pall of smoke advanced across South-East Asia, blocking out the sun for weeks, causing millions of people in Malaysia, Thailand, Cambodia, Vietnam and the Philippines as well as Indonesia to wear masks in frail defence against the polluted air.

The cause of the smoke was uncontrolled forest fires in the Indonesian part of the island of Borneo and in the Indonesian island of Sumatra. The cause of the fires, of the 'choking misery', as Andrew Higgins the *Guardian* correspondent put it, was the hunt for timber by companies – like that of Marquez in this story – pursuing profits while destroying the environment.

This ecological catastrophe, perhaps the greatest smog in history, will have caused immeasurable harm to plant and animal life in the region as well as to people. It reminds us of the interdependence of human beings and nature; and that we forget this at our peril. Muyu's war against the Yellow Giants has also to be our war.

JW

... if you liked this, you'll love these ...

Z FOR ZACHARIAH
Robert C. O'Brien

I am afraid. Someone is coming.

Ann Burden, the lone survivor of a nuclear holocaust, is threatened by the arrival in her valley of an unknown intruder. She hides, he watches and they both wait. Might he be a friend and ally, this scientist in a radiation-proof suit, or have the horrors he has witnessed turned him into something more sinister? The answer unfolds in a battle of wills which ends in a chilling struggle for survival, between a girl and the last man on earth.

'A stunning book ... not to be missed' – Observer

FALL-OUT
Gudrun Pausewang

As the radioactive fall-out from a leaking nuclear power station gets closer, the government's glib plans for coping with such a disaster collapse. Fourteen-year-old Janna, left alone to look after her little brother in a world gone mad with fear, must make the decisions which will mean life or death for both of them.

'A sobering but totally consuming novel by an excellent writer' – *Sunday Telegraph*

'Hard truths about the effects of fall-out make this book gripping, its message cannot be mistaken' – *School Library Journal*

... if you liked this, you'll love these ...

STONE COLD
Robert Swindells

Winner of the Carnegie Medal 1994 and the Sheffield Book Prize

Homeless, frightened and alone, Link finds himself down-and-out in London after fleeing from his brutish stepfather. He only survives because he's befriended by streetwise Ginger. When Ginger suddenly disappears, Link is in despair. Then he meets Gail, and even the cold doorways and hard pavements don't seem so bad. He even stops thinking about Ginger, but other kids are vanishing now. Intent on his grisly mission, the man who calls himself Shelter stalks his next victim. Will it be Link?

'A gripping, haunting tale' – *Publishing News*

FLOUR BABIES
Anne Fine

Winner of the Carnegie Medal and the Whitbread Children's Novel Award

When the annual school science fair comes round, Mr Cartwright's class don't get to work on the Soap Factory, the Maggot Farm or the Exploding Custard Tins. To their intense disgust they get the Flour Babies – sweet little six-pound bags of flour that must be cared for at all times. Young Simon Martin, a committed hooligan, approaches the task with little enthusiasm. But as the days pass, he not only grows fond of his flour baby, he also comes to learn more than he could have imagined about the pressures and strains of becoming a parent.

... if you liked this, you'll love these ...

JUNK
Melvin Burgess

Winner of the Carnegie Medal and winner of the Guardian Fiction Prize

Junk is Melvin Burgess's stunning and vivid depiction of young people in the grip of heroin addiction. The story is told in many different voices, from the addicts themselves to the friends watching from the outside who try to prevent tragedy. Junk is the most ambitious novel to date from this acclaimed writer. This book is unique in its unfailingly honest and realistic account of the realities of drug addiction and its ultimately tragic impact on the lives of addicts and those around them.

Junk is not suitable for readers under fourteen years old.

It contains descriptions of drug-taking and sex.

READ MORE IN PUFFIN

For children of all ages, Puffin represents quality and variety – the very best in publishing today around the world.

For complete information about books available from Puffin – and Penguin – and how to order them, contact us at the appropriate address below. Please note that for copyright reasons the selection of books varies from country to country.

On the worldwide web: www.puffin.co.uk

In the United Kingdom: Please write to *Dept. EP, Penguin Books Ltd, Bath Road, Harmondsworth, West Drayton, Middlesex UB7 0DA*

In the United States: Please write to *Consumer Sales, Penguin USA, P.O. Box 999, Dept. 17109, Bergenfield, New Jersey 07621-0120*. VISA and MasterCard holders call 1-800-253-6476 to order Penguin titles

In Canada: Please write to *Penguin Books Canada Ltd, 10 Alcorn Avenue, Suite 300, Toronto, Ontario M4V 3B2*

In Australia: Please write to *Penguin Books Australia Ltd, P.O. Box 257, Ringwood, Victoria 3134*

In New Zealand: Please write to *Penguin Books (NZ) Ltd, Private Bag 102902, North Shore Mail Centre, Auckland 10*

In India: Please write to *Penguin Books India Pvt Ltd, 706 Eros Apartments, 56 Nehru Place, New Delhi 110 019*

In the Netherlands: Please write to *Penguin Books Netherlands bv, Postbus 3507, NL-1001 AH Amsterdam*

In Germany: Please write to *Penguin Books Deutschland GmbH, Metzlerstrasse 26, 60594 Frankfurt am Main*

In Spain: Please write to *Penguin Books S. A., Bravo Murillo 19, 1° B, 28015 Madrid*

In Italy: Please write to *Penguin Italia s.r.l., Via Felice Casati 20, I–20124 Milano*

In France: Please write to *Penguin France S. A., 17 rue Lejeune, F–31000 Toulouse*

In Japan: Please write to *Penguin Books Japan, Ishikiribashi Building, 2–5–4, Suido, Bunkyo-ku, Tokyo 112*

In South Africa: Please write to *Longman Penguin Southern Africa (Pty) Ltd, Private Bag X08, Bertsham 2013*